IN LOVE AND WAR

IN LOVE AND WAR

BY
SANDRA WARD

HARLEQUIN
London · Toronto · New York · Sydney

All the characters in this book have no existence outside the imagination of the Author, and have no relation whatsoever to anyone bearing the same name or names. They are not even distantly inspired by any individual known or unknown to the Author, and all the incidents are pure invention.

The text of this publication or any part thereof may not be reproduced or transmitted in any form or by any means, electronic or mechanical, including photocopying, recording, storage in an information retrieval system, or otherwise, without the written permission of the publisher.

First published in Great Britain 1985 by Mills & Boon Limited 15–16 Brook's Mews, London W1A 1DR

© Sandra Ward 1985

Australian copyright 1985

ISBN 0 373 50207 9

Set in Linotron Times 10 on 10½pt. 20-0485-59,700

Photoset by Rowland Phototypesetting Ltd, Bury St Edmunds, Suffolk Made and printed in Great Britain by Richard Clay (The Chaucer Press) Ltd, Bungay, Suffolk

CHAPTER ONE

'I'M only Mr Cayhill's secretary, Catherine.' Sophia shook her head apologetically, her dark brown eyes and short black hair looking darker than normal under the indirect lighting in the restaurant. 'I wish I was in a position to help you . . . somehow, but I'm not.

'The bank has given you two extension on the note already,' she continued, her eyes on the stem of her water glass and not on the woman across the table from her. It was easier that way.

The facts, such as they were, were incredibly simple: Catherine Parker needed money, lots of it, and in a hurry—and she wasn't going to get it.

'Mr Cayhill doesn't have any choice,' Sophia continued. 'He couldn't give you any more time even if he wanted to. He's got a board of directors to answer to himself. Are you sure you can't raise the money somewhere else? I know you've tried, but . . .' She finally glanced at the unnaturally silent Catherine, only Catherine wasn't paying any attention to her, she was staring at something across the room.

'Catherine? Are you even listening to me?' She paused. 'You asked me what I thought Mr Cayhill was going to do about your note and I'm trying to answer you, but you're not paying any attention.' Sophia's expression puckered. Catherine looked pale to her, very pale—and her usually sparkling green eyes had a peculiar glassy look about them.

'*Catherine!*' Sophia reached for Catherine's arm, her voice raising anxiously as she did. 'Say something—anything!' she begged, giving Catherine's arm a quick shake. 'What is it? Tell me. You look like you've seen a ghost.'

Catherine turned and slowly looked at Sophia. A complete opposite to Sophia's dark, exotic good looks, Catherine's fair complexion was a natural complement to her fiery red hair and emerald green eyes. Only right now her fair complexion was so fair as to be white and her cat-like eyes were narrowed to mere slits of flashing green flame. 'I don't believe it!' She shook her head, the expression on her face mirroring the disbelief in her voice. 'After all these years, I can't believe he'd do this to me now!'

'Who? What?' The worried look on Sophia's face had gone, only to be replaced by confusion. 'Who are you talking about—Mr Cayhill at the bank? I know he did business with your father long before your father died and left you Parker Plastics to run, but he can't let past acquaintances influence his . . .' Sophia pinched her lips tightly; Catherine was vehemently shaking her head no. 'Well, if you're not talking about Mr Cayhill,' Sophia instinctively lowered her voice to a conspiratorial whisper, 'then who *are* you talking about?'

Catherine's response was a level green-eyed glare across the room. '*That man!*' she gritted, and her two-word statement was so filled with contempt that Sophia's eyes widened with surprise. Sophia had known Catherine for about two years now, and while most of their contact had been strictly business through the bank, they had lunched on occasion and Sophia had never heard that tone in Catherine's voice before.

More than curious, Sophia followed the direction of Catherine's livid glare, her own dark eyes coming to rest on an incredibly handsome man. Did Catherine mean him? As Sophia's eyes remained on the tall black-haired man, his steel grey suit and blinding white shirt accenting his tan and bringing out the grey of his eyes, her reaction was a natural one. When you saw something pleasing to the eye it generally made you smile. 'You don't mean him?' she smiled.

'I do,' Catherine replied, grim-faced and sober, her

already tight lips tightening more when she saw Sophia's pleased smile.

'Who is he?' Intrigued almost to the point of fascination, Sophia leaned over the table, her voice a curious murmur against the noisy bustle of the busy restaurant.

But before Catherine could reply she spun back to face Sophia, her hand flying to her face in what was clearly a moment of sheer panic. Whoever the man, was the sight of him just now had upset Catherine more than she wanted to let on. 'Oh, lord!' she gasped in a horse whisper. 'He's seen us and he's coming over. Don't talk to him!' This slightly bizarre order was hissed through her fingers. 'No matter what he wants, or what he says—ignore him. Pretend he's not there.'

'Ignore him?' Sophia almost laughed at Catherine's demand. 'You can't be serious, Catherine! Even if I agree to that, how could I possibly ignore anyone as beautiful as he is?' The man began to make his way slowly through the crowded restaurant towards them, the people ahead of him parting automatically as if by remote control or thought command. 'Who is he?' whispered Sophia, trying to comply with Catherine's demand by hiding with her hand the pleased smile that formed on her lips.

'It's *him!*' Catherine hissed impatiently through her teeth, as if 'him' was all the explanation necessary.

'Him? Him who?' Sophia was becoming desperate. 'You're not making any sense, Catherine. You've got to tell me more than "him"—"him" doesn't explain anything.' She suddenly stopped talking, the sound of her breath catching sharply in her throat telling Catherine what she didn't want to know. *Him* was at the table, his towering six-foot-plus frame and wide shoulders throwing imaginary as well as real shadows over women and table alike.

'Hello, Cat,' he drawled, his low masculine voice completing the picture of sheer animal magnetism. 'It's been a long time.' His grey eyes boldly admired

Catherine's good looks, his lips curving lazily into a pleased smile when he was through. 'How have you been?'

Catherine stubbornly stuck by her own demand: she neither looked up nor acknowledged his presence in any way, even though he was standing so close to her he was practically touching her shoulder. For one awful minute it looked as if she was actually going to ignore him—totally. Just leave him standing there talking to the top of her head.

It was an uncomfortable situation and growing more so, and Sophia, her eyes widening in a silent plea for Catherine to do something, began to wriggle nervously in her chair. It was obvious to anyone looking at this man that here was a man not accustomed to being ignored, especially as blatantly as Catherine was doing it. It was probably only one of many things he wouldn't tolerate.

From under the table came the scratching noise of a nervous high heel tapping against the floor. Catherine was desperately trying to pretend he wasn't there, but the very action of her tapping foot clearly demonstrated that his presence was very disturbing to her. Angry, she brought the offending foot to a halt. Drawing a deep breath and putting on her face a look of total indifference, she finally, reluctantly, turned her head and looked up at him, the sudden attack of butterflies being squelched instantly. 'Hello, Sadler,' she said tightly.

Sadler arched an eyebrow as he waited for Catherine to say something else, but she evidently had no intention of adding to her succinct greeting. She had done what was necessary and that was that. As each second continued to pass silently, his thick eyebrows grew more and more expressive, while his tapping hand on the back of Catherine's chair drew more than one poisonous glance from her. Unaffected, he just smiled. 'The years have been kind to you, Cat.' Smoky grey eyes raked her frame. 'You haven't changed.' His voice softened until it gave the impression that anyone listening to it was eavesdropping on a very private conversation. 'You still look good.'

'Don't sound so surprised, Sadler. There's no reason why I shouldn't—*now*,' Catherine smiled back icily, his compliment not drawing the customary 'thank you'. With a reluctant sigh she added begrudgingly, 'You haven't changed much either, Sadler. How have you been?' She asked the question, but it was clear she wasn't interested in the answer.

'Busy,' he answered, 'but I can't complain.' The more he talked the more obvious it became that his voice was a combination of softness and masculinity. It was a mesmerising voice and one you could listen to for ever. While this was perhaps true in Sophia's case, to Catherine the sound of his voice was an assault on her nerves, and her expression showed it.

'And it *has* been a long time,' he repeated, acknowledging her grimace with a sigh of his own. 'I'd really like to hear what you've been doing with yourself, but I . . .' he paused and glanced searchingly around the restaurant, 'I've got an engagement for lunch, but I must be early.' He smiled quickly and reached for the back of an empty chair at the table. 'Since that's the case I might be able to spare a few moments. May I?'

'Yes, please do.' Sophia's reply was emphatic, her dark eyes lingering in his direction.

Catherine's reply was also emphatic and just a little bit louder. '*No!*' She gave Sophia a warning glance before shaking her head at Sadler. 'I'm sorry, Sadler,' her lips formed a smile, but her eyes were as cold as ice, 'but it's just not convenient right now. Ironic, isn't it?' she waved her hand absently in mid-air. 'I remember how difficult it was for you to find time to spare a few minutes for me, and this time I can't spare any time for you.' She inclined her head towards Sophia. 'We're right in the middle of an important business lunch and I'm afraid I can't ask you to join us.' Her smile faded. 'But then I don't have to explain about business lunches to you, do I?'

'Still the shrew, eh, Cat?' He said the words very quietly, his grey eyes hardening slightly. 'I had hoped that maybe these past few years had taken some of the edge off your tongue, but I can see I was wrong.' He suddenly picked up her left hand, smiling to himself when he saw her ringless fingers. 'Not married?' He laughed as she snatched her hand out of his grip. 'I can't say I'm surprised. It would take a brave sort of man who would be willing to . . .'

'And you're still the perfect gentleman, aren't you, Sadler?' she snapped, feeling her cheeks burn and hating herself for the weakness. 'I'd like to return the compliment and say that I've thought of you these past few years and hoped that perhaps you might have changed—herculean task that that is—but I can't say that,' she smiled tightly, 'because frankly, Sadler, I haven't thought of you at all—in *any* respect.'

If Catherine had harboured a secret desire to upset him, she was instantly disappointed. 'In four years, Cat?' He put his head back and laughed, exposing perfectly straight white teeth. 'You haven't thought of me once, not once?' He shook his head lightly with disbelief. 'I find that just a little bit hard to believe.'

'That's only because you're an egotist, Sadler,' Catherine replied tartly. 'And stop calling me Cat. My name is Catherine.'

'I'm not an egotist, Cat,' he answered slowly, ignoring her demand to be called Catherine. 'Not at all. I like to think of myself as a realist, and it's simply not realistic to believe that you haven't thought of me once in four years.'

He didn't wait for Catherine to reply but dismissed her totally by glancing at Sophia and giving her a warm attractive smile. Charming and well-practised, it nevertheless drew a delighted smile from Sophia. 'Cat's manners always were atrocious.' He held out a strong, darkly tanned hand, the back of which was covered with fairly liberal sprinkling of coarse black hair. 'I'm Sadler

McQuade—and you're—?'

'Speechless.' Sophia's blurted reply was promptly rewarded with another of his flashing white smile. 'Sophia,' she continued softly, 'Sophia Blair.' She held out her hand and Sadler took it, holding on to it just a few seconds longer than necessary.

Catherine had seen that smile and handshake before and knew the effect it could have on women, and Sophia was obviously no exception. For women Sadler had *that* smile and for men it was a pleasant nod and firmer shake, but no matter who he was dealing with Sadler always managed to come out on top.

'How do you do?' purred Sophia silkily.

'Better than most, actually,' he replied, finally releasing Sophia's hand. From anyone else this reply might have sounded smug, but not from Sadler. He had no need to brag about anything—his was an honest reply to Sophia's question.

It was also a reply that brought a rather nasty curl to Catherine's lip.

Sadler glanced at his watch, a handsome gold band that circled his wide wrist. 'I'm sorry, ladies,' he smiled apologetically. 'As *charming* as this has been,' he gave Catherine a quick glance, 'I'm afraid I must be leaving. Cat—Sophia,' he acknowledged each girl with a nod and a flashing smile. Then with a final curious glance in Catherine's direction, he turned and walked away, the waters of humanity parting ahead of him the same way they had when he approached them.

'Who was that?' Sophia's eyes danced with growing interest as she watched Sadler's broad grey-suited back walk away from them. Head and shoulders above everyone else in the restaurant—Sophia's eyes weren't the only pair of mascaraed eyes in the room following him. 'I don't think I've ever seen anyone that good-looking . . . and that smile,' she sighed deeply. 'The man gives me goose-pimples just thinking about him!'

'Caps,' Catherine replied tartly. Her eyes also were on

his disappearing back, but the look on her face wasn't the same adoring expression as the one on Sophia's.

'What did you say?' Sophia tore her gaze away from Sadler long enough to give Catherine a distracted look.

'Caps.' This time Catherine tapped her front teeth with her fingernail.

'Oh, they're not!' Sophia refused to believe her. 'But he was so perfect,' her voice faded wistfully, her eyes lingering on his profile. 'He wouldn't have caps. He couldn't!'

Catherine made a little face and relented. 'No,' she frowned, 'they're not caps, they're real. But they should be caps,' she snarled. 'Nobody has a right to be as totally "perfect" as Sadler McQuade is, and that includes his teeth.'

'Oh?' Sophia's dark eyes narrowed suspiciously. 'And how do you know that they *are* real and not caps?' Her voice was mildly inquisitive. 'Just how well do you know him, and *who is he*?'

'I just told you who he is,' Catherine replied with a gesture, then she made another face and scowled. 'No, that's wrong,' she shook her head. 'I didn't tell you who he was, he did that himself. Sadler never was one to cover his light with a bushel.'

Sophia drew a deep, loud, exasperated breath and stared pointedly at Catherine. 'He told me his name is Sadler McQuade. You told me those are his real teeth and not caps, and *that*,' she tossed up her hands in frustration, 'is the total extent of what I know about Sadler McQuade. Except,' she glanced in his direction, 'he's quite possibly the handsomest man I've ever met. Or have I already said that?' she laughed.

'You have,' answered Catherine, neither agreeing nor denying Sophia's observation.

'Oh. Well,' she gave Catherine a threatening look, 'are you going to tell me who he is, or am I going to be forced to choke the information out of you?'

'All right,' Catherine gave in. 'Who he is and always

will be is Sadler McQuade.' She sighed softly, her green eyes and pale eyebrows suddenly expressive. 'Who he was was my husband. Once upon a time we were married . . . to each other,' she added bitterly.

'Married?' Sophia's mouth fell open. Whatever she thought Catherine had been going to say, it certainly wasn't that! 'You were married to him?'

'Distasteful idea, isn't it?' Catherine shrugged apologetically.

'Hardly distasteful. Sadler McQuade is gorgeous.' Sophia's dark lashes curled across her cheek as she tried—unsuccessfully—to take another look at the man under discussion without Catherine noticing. 'Unless he's undergone recent radical plastic surgery,' she added, 'I suppose he looked like that when you were married to him.'

'More or less,' admitted Catherine, her voice fading slowly as memories of that time came flooding back, memories she had tried for the past four years to keep pushed to the back of her mind. 'The silver streaks over his ears are new,' she observed weakly, not turning to look at him. She didn't have to—every feature, every detail, every new line was crystal clear in her mind. 'Anybody else would turn grey,' she added dryly, 'but that's not Sadler's style. His hair has to turn *silver*. Everything else about him is the same,' she concluded tightly, 'including the stuffed shirt.'

That was a matter of opinion, and Sophia's eyes widened as she leaned over the table, the better to hear what Catherine was about to say. 'Well?' she paused. 'What happned? I didn't know you'd ever been married. You don't go by the name McQuade.'

'Certainly not!' Catherine's green eyes flared. 'I wanted nothing from him after the divorce—not his money, not even his name. I . . .' her voice cracked slightly as if she was struggling with the words, 'I took my maiden name of Parker back.

'And not too many people know I was married,' she

continued, the tone of her voice relaying to Sophia that that was how she wanted to keep it. 'It's not something I care to brag about. I . . . I was nineteen at the time,' she smiled bitterly. 'Married *and* divorced all at the tender age of nineteen. As far as marriages go—even these days—it was a short one. Eight months, to be exact,' she frowned. 'Give or take a few hundred years.'

She sighed and stared vacantly in mid-air. It all seemed so long ago to her, and yet talking about it to Sophia brought it all back as if it was only yesterday. Meeting Sadler, their marriage, their divorce and finally the death of her father . . . and now seeing Sadler again. It had gone full circle.

'This is really none of my business,' Sophia's voice pulled Catherine back to the present. 'And you certainly don't have to tell me, I'll understand—but what happened?'

For a moment it looked as if Catherine might not talk about it, then she changed her mind and shrugged indifferently. 'I don't mind . . . it was a long time ago and it doesn't matter now. For a while, I'll admit, Sadler and I were happy. We were . . .' She suddenly stopped talking and frowned, her cool green gaze flashing to the man on the other side of the room. Why explain with words when a practical demonstration could do much better? 'Take a good look at Sadler,' she suggested in flat tones. 'Try not to drool and tell me what you think might have gone wrong with the marriage.'

From Sophia's almost instant glance at Sadler it was clear she needed no added encouragement to look at him, in fact it was obvious she was having trouble *not* doing it.

And why not? Sadler McQuade was tall, broad-shouldered, with slim hips and jet black hair that waved on the top and curled tantalisingly over the tops of his ears and the back of his neck. And his eyes were smoky-grey, not dark and not light, but a wispy grey that changed colour with every new situation.

As Sophia's gaze left Sadler and went slowly around the room, the answer to Catherine's puzzle came easily to mind. Sadler was drawing more attention than just hers. 'Ah,' she nodded knowingly. 'Another woman—it has to be.'

Catherine laughed, but it wasn't the sound of a person amused. 'You're on the right track, Sophia, but you've got to increase your scope, think bigger. And I don't mean a *big* woman.'

Sophia's eyes widened. 'Wo*men*?'

'Right!' Catherine pinched her lips together, drawing out the word in a tight hiss. 'I couldn't compete with his harem,' her expression hardened visibly. 'I *wouldn't* compete. When it got too much for me to handle, I divorced him.'

'*You* divorced *him*?' Sophia was surprised and a soft whistle escaped her lips. 'That must have been messy.' That thought put a new look of concern on her face.

'On the contrary,' Catherine's shrug of indifference was obviously feigned, 'it was quick and clean.'

'But not painless,' Sophia added gently.

'No, not painless,' Catherine shook her head slowly, her admission putting a look of pain on her face. It was without a doubt the worst time in her life. 'Sadler didn't contest the divorce,' she continued. 'He was at a point in his career where he was just making a name for himself. I suppose he realised that if it went to court it would have been messy and maybe tarnish his image. I didn't ask for anything from him, so there was really no point in his fighting it.' A bitterness crept into her voice. 'Nothing. Not his name, not his money. It was over—period—and the only thing I wanted from him was out!'

'Still . . .' Sophia's gaze kept returning to Sadler, 'it couldn't have been an easy time for you. Maybe if I'd been around at the time I could have consoled him. *You*, I mean, of course,' she forced a laugh, but Catherine knew exactly what Sophia meant.

'I'm afraid you would have had to stand at the end of

the line to comfort Sadler,' Catherine replied tightly, irrationally irritated that Sophia's attention kept wandering in Sadler's direction. Sophia had a look on her face that Catherine had seen dozens—no, *hundreds* of times before. At first it had been flattering to realise that your husband was attractive to other women. It made you feel good to think that you were the one he had married over everyone else. But when the furtive glances turned to bold advances and in some cases outright propositions, it wasn't funny any more. It was hell.

'Good grief!' Sophia, her eyes still on the other side of the room, gasped with open surprise. 'Where's the rest of that woman's dress?'

Grateful to have something to think about other than Sadler, Catherine looked quickly and discovered the subject of Sophia's dismay. Just walking into the restaurant and drawing quite a bit of eye attention herself, both male and female, stood a tall willowy blonde wearing a dress cut so low in the front it appeared to defy gravity. One good healthy sneeze and . . .

'Hmmm,' Sophia turned back to Catherine, a sober, thoughtful look on her face, 'I wonder how I'd look in a dress like that—a different colour, of course.'

'Of course!' Catherine couldn't help but laugh at the serious expression on Sophia's face. 'You've got the shape, but do you really think you've got the nerve to . . .' She stopped talking and laughing, a sudden thought bringing a new frown to her delicate features. 'What do you want to bet that that woman is Sadler's "lunch engagement"?'

'Are you kidding?' Sophia was impressed. 'You really think so?' The words were barely out of Sophia's mouth when the semi-clad blonde spotted Sadler and smiled— the kind of smile that went with brown paper wrappers.

'What did I tell you?' But Catherine's victorious smile put a bitter taste in her mouth, and narrow-eyed she watched the blonde slither over to Sadler's table. He smiled as he rose to greet her, but somehow his smile didn't stop with the blonde. Looking over her shoulder, Sadler let his smile travel across the restaurant and land squarely on Catherine's sour expression. Her reaction was automatic if not well thought out—she stuck her tongue out at him.

Catherine's reaction was evidently everything Sadler had hoped for and more, for his smile grew instantly into a soft laugh, a low soft laugh that the blonde naturally thought was for her benefit alone. The results were disastrous as far as Catherine was concerned, for the blonde turned the steam on and, furious, Catherine tore her eyes away, her hands tightening into angry, white-knuckled fists at either side of her place mat.

'Do you want to leave?' Sophia's understanding question restored a little calm to Catherine's frayed nerves. 'I can see you're upset,' Sophia continued gently. 'And who wouldn't be—seeing your ex after all these years, *and* with another woman. We don't have to eat here, Catherine,' she shook her head. 'We can go somewhere else. It's not a problem, we haven't even ordered yet.'

The suggestion was tempting, very much so, and Catherine considered it, but only for a moment. 'No,' she quickly refused, 'why should we? I'm not going to let Sadler run me out of this restaurant—or anywhere else, for that matter. He'd *love* that,' her lip curled. 'He'd love to see me get up right now and leave. Well, I'm not going to. I'm going to stay right here and enjoy my lunch, even if I choke on it. If Sadler's uncomfortable here with me and doesn't like it, then let him leave. As far as I'm concerned Sadler and his "lunch engagement" don't even exist.'

'Uh-huh,' Sophia agreed, at least vocally, but it didn't take a genius to see that Catherine was struggling to keep up a brave front. 'Why haven't you mentioned him before now?'

'Out of sight—out of mind.' Catherine's flip answer was indifferent, but her reply had been too quick and too bitter to be truly indifferent. 'When I told him I wanted a divorce, he left the States. Probably for South America,' she added coolly. 'I haven't been sufficiently interested to keep up with his whereabouts, but Argentina would be a good guess. He has a "friend" down there, if you know what I mean.'

Sophia did, and the intriguing look in her eye said so. 'I suppose that's why he's so tan. I wonder if he's tan all over?'

'Who cares!' Catherine snapped, Sophia's interest in Sadler had gone beyond simple curiosity. She was about to take her place in line at Sadler's feet and her constant yammering about Sadler was driving Catherine crazy.

'Catherine!' Sophia looked surprised by her outburst. 'Does it really bother you to talk about him?'

'No,' Catherine smiled, and lied. 'Why should it? I told you—it's over and forgotten.'

'OK,' nodded Sophia, taking Catherine at her word. 'So tell me why you think he went to South America, or was it because of his "friend"?'

'No, not really,' Catherine replied sourly. 'Sadler owns a ranch in Argentina. Cattle, I think.'

'You think?' Sophia's dark eyebrows arched. 'Don't you know? How could you be married to him for a year and not know . . .'

'Eight months!' Catherine interrupted sharply. 'We were married for eight months—not a year.'

'Whatever!' Sophia waved her hand irritably. 'The point I'm making, or trying to make, is how could you be married to him for whatever length of time, and not know what he does for a living? Or did he buy the ranch in Argentina after you and he . . .'

'No, no.' Catherine's eyes and voice hardened. 'Sadler had the ranch when we were married. I was there once,' she added bitterly, her eyes narrowing strangely when she looked at Sophia. 'You remind me a little bit of someone . . .' Her voice faded into oblivion. Obviously that was something she hadn't meant to say.

'It's a big ranch,' she continued in a normal voice. 'Several thousand acres, and he raises beef cattle.'

'Of course,' Catherine continued slowly, all her attention fixed on Sophia and her reaction to what she was about to say next. 'That's only a part, a very *small* part, of what Sadler does for a living.' She paused again. 'Sadler McQuade is *the* McQuade of McQuade Electronics. Ever hear of him?'

'Have I?' Sophia's dark eyes gleamed. 'He's one of the wealthiest men around . . . and so good-looking,' she cooed. 'What a combination! Ah,' she gasped lightly, 'do you think that blonde's his wife?'

The look of alarm on Sophia's face was so transparent that Catherine couldn't help but laugh, and this time it was with real humour. 'You can't be serious! Sadler tie himself down to only one woman? That's like trying to eat only one potato chip—it just can't be done. After the divorce I even told him he was free to marry as many women as he wanted to. I thought that would make him a very happy man.'

'And didn't it?'

'I'm not sure,' Catherine frowned deeply, an uncertain note creeping into her voice. 'Yes, I *am* sure,' she abruptly changed her mind. 'That must have been exactly what Sadler wanted, because after I told him that, he said to me, "Cat"—and this is a direct quote—"Cat, my marriage to you was my first, last and only marriage. I'll never get married again."'

'So,' Catherine forced a tiny smile, 'to finally answer your question about the blonde—no, I don't think she's his wife. Once Sadler was unencumbered he meant to play the field again. He's not going to give up his freedom again for anyone.'

'Oh?' Sophia didn't look convinced. 'Are you sure that's what he meant?' One dark eyebrow arched sceptically. 'It sounds to me as if he was saying he would always consider himself married to you. Some people do that, you know.'

'That's nuts.' Catherine scoffed it off. 'You don't know Sadler or you wouldn't say that. That was only one of his little zingers. I always assumed that what he meant was that after one disastrous marriage he wouldn't be bothered with another one. Although,' she paused and scowled her displeasure, 'if anyone's got the right to be sour on marriage, it's me, not Sadler. He did the perfect job on me and I'm going to make sure I think twice before I make *that* mistake again. If I ever do.'

'Which mistake is that?' asked Sophia. 'Getting married or—' she paused, 'marrying someone you're afraid you can't hold on to, because that's what it sounds like to me. Did you try, Catherine? Eight months doesn't seem long enough,' she added quickly, talking over Catherine's attempt at a strangled rebuttal. 'Did you *really* try?'

'I tried—and eight months was *plenty* of time.' Catherine thinned her lips and stared at the inquisitive dark-eyed girl opposite her. She had no intention of going into the intimate details of her marriage with Sophia or anyone else. In fact she hadn't intended to ever mention Sadler's name again and she wouldn't have—if he hadn't suddenly showed up in the restaurant today. After all this time it came as a surprise to Catherine to discover it still hurt, and that painful self-betrayal was going to take some long, hard dealing with on a very personal level—certainly *not* with Sophia.

Catherine glanced down at the menu in her hand. 'I think I'll have the salad,' she smiled, and changed the subject. 'That looks good—and maybe an iced tea.'

'So,' Sophia was displeased, but she hid it well, 'you're not going to talk about him now—why not? A moment ago you were all too eager to tell me about your ex's faults. Are we about to get into something a little more touchy—like what you did wrong?'

Catherine didn't reply, but instead concentrated on her menu. She should never have started talking about Sadler in the first place, but then *she* didn't—it had been

Sophia. Slowly Catherine let her gaze go above the menu to Sophia—not surprisingly Sophia wasn't looking at her, she was looking at Sadler. And smiling to herself—with a look on her face like that of a child looking into a candy store window for the very first time. There were so many goodies, and all in one place, that she didn't know where to start first.

'What are you thinking about?' Catherine's icy probe betrayed a familiar stab of jealousy. But she didn't have to ask Sophia that question, she already knew the answer.

Caught daydreaming by Catherine's unexpected demand, Sophia smiled guiltily. 'Oh, nothing,' she shrugged, pretending to study the menu. 'I was thinking I'll get that salad, too. Summer's coming and I want to look good in my summer clothes.'

'Hmm.' Catherine accepted Sophia's answer with as much enthusiasm on her part as there was honesty in replying on Sophia's part. It was a little ironic, Catherine thought with a humourless smile, that both of them had something on their minds that they didn't want to discuss, and oddly enough that *some*thing was the *same* thing—Sadler McQuade.

Loathing herself for doing it, but unable to stop, Catherine went back to thinking about Sadler and their marriage. Sophia wasn't the only one fantasising about Sadler, only in Catherine's case fantasy had become reality . . . at least for a little while. If marriages could be rated solely on performance in the bedroom then theirs had been a roaring success. Only marriage was a lot more then that. It was the day-to-day dullness, and the night after night of sitting alone wondering where Sadler really was when he said he was working, and the unexpected out-of-town business trips that Sadler insisted on taking alone.

It was the past four years of telling yourself to forget Sadler and really believing that you had—only to realise in one split second that you hadn't forgotten at all.

Nothing. Not the soft way he had of holding her close and kissing her after they had made love, or the grey eyes that smiled at her in the mornings from the pillow next to her telling her everything would be all right, and she believed it. Making her believe that their marriage was forever, but forever was only eight months.

Bedevilled by her own thoughts, Catherine ran her hand across her forehead, an attempt perhaps to exorcise the demon Sadler. 'I hate you, Sadler,' she said the words silently to herself, his unsmiling image locked at the front of her mind.

Only Catherine hadn't spoken the words to herself, and a startled Sophia glanced up. The look on her face was one of sympathy and concern for Catherine, but there was something else in her expression that she tried to hide behind the slowly re-raised menu. It was something that had Catherine seen it, she would have recognised it instantly. It was the soft enigmatic smile, the slowly widening pupils, the racing pulse—it was a normal reaction to a physical stimulant.

But what kind of stimulant—sexual attraction, or too much pepper? Lunch was still more than twenty minutes away, but Sadler McQuade was just on the other side of the room.

CHAPTER TWO

It was three in the morning, and like a kitten Catherine sat curled up on one end of the living-room sofa, her silky red shoulder-length hair in wild disarray across the back of the cushion. Wide-eyed, restless and unable to sleep, Catherine had finally given up trying and had taken to prowling round her apartment in the dark, but even that did no good. She simply brought her thoughts with her.

And that was part of her problem—if not all of it. If she was going to sit here in the middle of the night worrying about something, then it should be how was she going to save her father's business and come up with the small but necessary miracle needed to save Parker Plastics from going bankrupt, and *not* to be here thinking about Sadler McQuade. Time was running out for Parker Plastics, and the only thing she could think about was Sadler.

Sadler McQuade. Just the sound of his name in her mind brought back every gesture, every word spoken or thought, every detail of their accidental meeting today in the restaurant. Why? Why did he have to come back to West Virginia *now*, of all times? Didn't she have enough to worry about without worrying if, or when, she was going to run into him again?

Her fingers curled into tight little fists at her sides. Why couldn't he stay in Argentina, or Antarctica, or wherever he'd been for the past four years? She put her head back and stared bleakly at the shifting shadows on the ceiling. Strangely shaped shadows caused by the intermittent coming through the blinds at the window. Thin grey slivers of light having neither a beginning nor an end—like herself, she thought bleakly. She had just spent four years trying to get rid of Sadler's memory and the stormy, sometimes savage emotions he could stir within her—and yet here she was, she sighed, thinking about Sadler again.

For a while, though, Catherine had had a certain amount of success putting Sadler out of her life, but she had managed to do that so well that aside from the turmoil surrounding her father's unexpected death, she had created for herself an emotional void. It was a fact that went neither unnoticed nor ignored by the few men she had dated. Cold and unfeeling had been the polite version of their opinion of Catherine, but they were wrong. Catherine was neither of those things—she was simply afraid. It was the deep down indescribable fear of being hurt again and out of instinctive self-preservation all of her emotions had been put on 'hold'. They were still there, but logic told her she couldn't be hurt again if she didn't *feel* anything.

The living-room light suddenly burst with electric stark-white life and startled her, her eyes going instantly to the wall switch and the man standing next to it. Hands on his hips, an unhappy, just-woken-up scowl on his face, he stared back at her. 'Why are you still up?' I thought we said goodnight five hours ago?' He yawned sleepily and rubbed at his eyes. 'Do you know it's past three o'clock?'

'I know.' Catherine's moment of being startled was over, and frowning to herself she drew a light breath and scrunched back down into the corner of the sofa. 'I've been sitting here listening to the clock tick off every second for the past three hours.'

Her eyes still on the man in the doorway, Catherine's pale brows drew together in mild consternation. 'Where'd you get those pyjamas?' She made a face. 'They're awful!'

'*You* gave them to me for Christmas two years ago,' he reminded her, grinning broadly when he heard her groan of acute dismay. 'And stop trying to change the subject and answer me—*why* are you still up?'

Catherine sighed and toyed idly with the folds in her long cotton nightgown. 'I can't sleep, Smitty,' she shook her head slowly, her voice filled with worry and uncertainty.

'Why not?'

'You're a good one to ask me that,' she glanced up sharply. 'You know the answer as well as I do.'

The grey-haired man frowned to himself as he squared his slightly stooping shoulders. Charles Smithson—Smitty—had known Catherine for a great many years, coming to work for her father after her mother had died when Catherine was only three. Wounded in World War Two, Smitty had remained in the Service until he could retire, taking the job with Catherine's father as a means of helping himself adjust from the military life to civilian. It was originally intended to be 'temporary' while his old friend Andrew Parker looked for a woman to help him care for little Catherine. Only 'temporary' became 'permanent' as Catherine's father slowly turned to his business to help him compensate for the loss of his wife. It became Smitty's job to take care of the skinned knees and bruised elbows and generally hug away Catherine's pain—only this was one pain he couldn't fix that easily. 'I suppose,' he frowned, 'You're upset about the business?'

'Of course I'm upset about the business!' Catherine's eyes flashed. 'Who in their right mind wouldn't be? I have exactly three days to come up with the money—*all* of it—or sit back and watch the bank throw a padlock on the front door.'

'I know all that,' Smitty flipped his hand as if knocking it aside as unimportant. 'But this is the first time it's made you get up in the middle of the night.' His wise eyes widened. 'I can't help but wonder if that's all that's on your mind?'

'Don't you think that's enough to keep *anybody* awake?' Her expression narrowed warily.

'Sure it is, but don't ask me,' he shrugged easily. 'You're the one who's been walking around here talking to herself ever since you came home from work today. Something else is bothering you, Catherine.' It wasn't a question, but a statement. 'Do you want to talk about it now and get it off your chest? You know I'll only find out what it is sooner or later.'

Catherine pursed her lips and widened her eyes defiantly. 'No.'

'Fine by me,' he dismissed her refusal with a wide grin. 'But if you're not going to talk about it then how about some warm milk? That'll help you get back to sleep.'

'Yuck!' She made a face. 'How about a gin and tonic instead?' she grinned. 'That will help me get to sleep too.'

'No. You're too young for a gin and tonic. Come on—get up,' his expression demanded she do just that. 'It's a glass of warm milk or nothing.'

'I'm twenty-three years old, in case you've forgotten,' she told him firmly, getting slowly to her feet. 'I wouldn't call that young.'

'OK,' he agreed, 'so you're ancient. But it's still going to be warm milk.'

Catherine smiled to herself as she followed Smitty down the hallway towards the kitchen. In a way she had had two fathers while she'd been growing up. One who might virtually ignore her for weeks at a time, then in a fit of guilt and remorse, indulge her with the wildest extravagances. And the other father—Smitty—who would quietly remove most of them and give her the things she really needed—stability, affection, attention.

'Did I really give you those pyjamas for Christmas?' Catherine still couldn't believe that she had actually bought Smitty grey silk pyjamas with tiny red hearts on them. 'They're terrible!' she began to laugh. 'No wonder I haven't seen you in them before now.' All of a sudden she stopped laughing and frowned. '*Why* haven't I seen you wearing them before now?'

He glanced over his shoulder at her. 'That's probably because I save them for special occasions.'

'Special occasions?' Catherine puzzled the date for a moment. 'What's so special about today?'

'Wash day,' he replied. 'The rest of my pyjamas are in the wash.' He stopped walking and pointed to one of the red stools at the counter. 'Slide up there and you can talk to me while I warm up your milk.'

'Smitty . . .' Catherine's slim shoulders seemed to droop with the weight of the world, 'I'm going to have to do something about the company, but I don't know what to do. I had lunch with Sophia today,' she frowned lightly, 'but she couldn't tell me anything that Mr Cayhill hasn't already told me. The bank can't give me any more extensions and I can't come up with the money. Not even a small part of what I owe. They want their money,' she shrugged philosophically, 'and I suppose I really can't blame them.'

'I can see where I've got three choices,' she continued, smiling briefly as she took the mug of hot cocoa from Smitty and saw the extra large dollop of freshly whipped cream on the top. 'I could sell the company outright, which is highly unlikely because I doubt if I could find a buyer, what with the financial shape it's in. Or I could merge with another company or a conglomerate interested in acquiring a small plastics business like ours— but again,' she added in dull tones, 'who wants to merge with a failing business? We're not exactly a prime takeover candidate. Unless,' she made a face, 'someone's purposely looking for a tax loss, in which case the company would probably go out of business anyway. And last but not least,' she drew a long, sad deep breath, 'I can close the doors and file bankruptcy myself, which is by far the least desireable choice, but the most probable one.'

Smitty sat and waited, watching her slowly sip her hot cocoa. 'So . . .' he drawled, 'what *are* you going to do?'

'Well—' Catherine's green eyes momentary flared

with renewed determination. She was by nature a fighter, and this was certainly a fight. 'First thing in the morning I'm going to see Mr Cayhill at the bank, on my hands and knees if I have to, *anything* to persuade him to give me another extension. Somehow I have to—I can't let everything my father worked so hard for go down the drain without putting up a struggle. After Mother died that business was his whole life, Smitty. I know that, and I owe at least that much.'

'Why?' Smitty's question was out before he could stop it. 'Forget I said that,' he quickly tried to wave it aside, smiling tenderly at a rather forlorn-looking Catherine. 'Let me put it a little differently. Ever since your father died and left you the company you've *been* trying to put it back on its feet. Maybe it's time you faced the cold, hard truth, Catherine.' He covered her hand lightly with his. 'You can't breathe fresh life into something that's dead. Parker Plastics is dead—it's a thing of the past.'

'No, Smitty,' Catherine shook her head in a vehement denial, 'I can't believe that—I *won't* believe that. I know Parker's is only a small commercial plastics company, but it's worth saving. With a fresh influx of capital we could have a successful business again. We . . .' her voice faltered under Smitty's steady but understanding gaze. 'All right,' she shrugged a shoulder, 'so we have a small cash flow problem, but we've had a little bad luck lately, and . . .'

'Bad luck doesn't have anything to do with it, Catherine,' Smitty cut in sharply. 'What you had was a father who spent half his life with his head in the clouds. It was either feast or famine with Andrew Parker, and virtually nothing in between. I knew your father for a long time, Catherine, and I liked him, but I wasn't blind to his faults. Andrew was generous beyond belief, when he had it. And when he didn't, he didn't worry about it. You can't live on the fat times for ever, you've got to plan for some lean in there somewhere.

'And I don't know that you *owe* him anything,' he

continued soberly. 'You've given it three years now, you can't go on spending the rest of your life worrying about a business that can't be saved.' Smitty shook his head slowly. 'What you need is a husband and a family to worry about, and maybe . . .'

'I've *had* a husband, thank you,' Catherine drew her lips tightly against her teeth, 'and you can see what that got me—nothing!'

'Yes, that's right,' his voice hardened, 'you did have a husband, but I can't help but wonder if you had put *half* the effort into saving your marriage that you have into trying to save your father's business, if things wouldn't have turned out differently for you and Sadler.'

'Sadler . . .' Catherine repeated his name very softly, very slowly. 'I saw Sadler today, Smitty.'

'Aha!' Smitty nodded his greying head knowingly. 'So that's what all this restlessness is about.' He paused. 'How is he?'

'The same,' Catherine made a little face, 'only more so—you know Sadler.'

'I wonder what he's doing back here in Charleston?' Smitty grunted thoughtfully to himself. 'Did he say?'

'No, he didn't, and I didn't ask him. It was hard enough just seeing him again without getting into any lengthy personal discussion with him. Besides,' she paused, 'he had a date.' Suddenly very tired, she put her nearly empty mug of cocoa down on the counter and stood up. 'I think I'll go back to bed now, Smitty,' she sighed. 'I'm tired.'

'Uh-huh,' Smitty drawled slowly, bringing her to a halt when she heard the note of scepticism in his voice.

'What's *that* supposed to mean?' she asked, glancing back over her shoulder. 'I can't tell you anything more about Sadler than that. We barely exchanged half a dozen words, and most of them were unpleasant.'

'I didn't say that you could,' Smitty looked totally innocent of any implied crime. '*Uh-huh* is merely a catch-all expression that I used to reply to your statement—that's all it was. It doesn't have to *mean* anything.'

'Uh-huh!' Catherine didn't believe that for a minute.

'*See!*' Smitty smiled smugly.

She turned and headed once again for her bedroom. 'Good night, Smitty.'

'Good night, Catherine.'

The hot West Virginia sun beat down on Catherine as she slowly parked her car in the lot next to the neat, redbrick building of Parker Plastics. At one time—and not all that long ago either—all the parking spaces in the lot had had employees' cars in them. But that wasn't true any more. Most of the employees had quit, and the ones that were left were the older employees, the men and women who had been with her father the longest. The ones who might have the most difficulty finding new jobs and subsequently the ones who had the most to loose if Parker's went bankrupt. This handful of employees was Catherine's responsibility now, for they literally depended on her for their livelihood. Not a comforting thought at the best of times, and certainly not now under these circumstances.

A long silky strand of red hair slipped free and landed on her cheek. For a moment she did nothing about it, then with a bone-weary sigh she brushed it—and the tear behind it—aside. Oh, Mr Cayhill had been pleasant enough, and quite sympathetic. After all, he had smiled, hadn't he done business with her father for many years? But in this case he had to be adamant. He was terribly, terribly sorry, of course, but the bank was in no position to give her any more extensions. Times were difficult for banks as well as small businesses, and he would have to *insist* on the monies owed, as if *insisting* alone would accomplish what Catherine had been unable to do up to now. If that was the case, she frowned humourlessly, she would have *insisted* years ago.

As she walked across the small patch of neatly mowed

dark green grass that bordered the front of the building, she had a bone-chilling feeling that this was going to be the last time she would ever set foot inside Parker Plastics. The strange feeling persisted, and she came to a stop, staring reassuringly at the building before she walked on, still trying to shake the ominous sense of gloom as she did.

She was being ridiculous, she told herself firmly. The meeting at the bank hadn't gone in her favour and she was letting it depress her, that's all it was. She still had most of three days to come up with the money, and come up with it she would!

Putting on what she hoped was a don't-worry-everything-will-be-all-right smile, Catherine opened one of the large double glass doors and walked inside. Summer was officially a few weeks away, but the weather was already sweltering and the air-conditioned atmosphere inside the building was a welcome relief.

Catherine's office was up the short flight of stairs and to the right of the front door. It had been her father's office and she had naturally taken it over when she took over Parker's. On her father's death Catherine's legacy had amounted to a strange assortment—to say the least. Besides her father's office, the company and all of its debts, she had inherited a handful of worried employees, Smitty—who had been more like a father to her than her real father had—and Maggie.

Prim, neat and wearing glasses that made her look older than her fifty-plus years, Maggie glanced up at the sound of the opening door, saw it was Catherine and smiled. 'Well? How did it go at the bank? Did you have any luck with Mr Cayhill? Did he agree to . . .' She let her voice fade slowly as Catherine's expression began to change. 'Never mind,' Maggie shook her head and sighed. 'I think I already know the answer to that one. The bank said no.'

'The bank said no.' Catherine collapsed in the big black leather chair behind her father's desk. The large chair and even larger antique oak desk combined to give the impression that she was much younger than her twenty-three years, an illusion that didn't always work to her favour. Anyone looking at Catherine now would be reminded of the pigtailed, red-haired, freckled-nosed little girl who would come with her father to work and 'play' office—only Catherine wasn't playing any more.

'Mr Cayhill said no,' she repeated. 'Oh, he was very nice about it,' she continued, waving her hand absently in mid-air. 'And very sympathetic. The bank wants its money—all of it. In three days, Maggie,' she sighed deeply, 'unless a minor miracle occurs, the bank will be forced to foreclose and attach the property. Not a very pleasant idea,' her delicate features hardened, 'Parker Plastics going on the auction block.

'I'm running out of ideas and time.' Her green eyes reflected for the first time a concession to defeat. 'What I need now is a fairy godmother.' She smiled sadly at Maggie. 'Know of any?'

'Not offhand,' Maggie shook her head soberly. 'Didn't Mr Cayhill have a suggestion—besides the fairy godmother thing, I mean?'

'Sure.' Catherine sat back in her father's chair and pursed her lips. 'All I have to do is find someone with more money than brains, who's willing to come in sight unseen, pay off the note at the bank, re-finance it so I can start all over again to pay it off while I try and turn the business around.' She made a face. 'I think I'd have more luck finding a fairy godmother!'

'Oh, Catherine,' Maggie slowly shook her head, her short brown heavily sprayed hair staying perfectly, almost plastically, in place. 'If you haven't been able to do that in the past few years,' she pointed out gently, 'then why do you think you can do it in the next three days? Or three months, or three more years for that matter. Accept it, Catherine, the bitter truth is that Parker's can't be saved.'

'Do you know you're beginning to sound like Smitty?'

Catherine's eyes widened expressively. 'But just in case you've forgotten, we're talking about *your* job too, Maggie, or don't you like all the little things being gainfully employed provides—like *food*?'

'Sure I do,' Maggie shrugged easily. 'But I'm not so old that I can't find another job. I'm a damn good secretary. Besides,' she grinned and ran her hands down her tailored hips, 'I'm not all that bad looking. Maybe I can find somebody filthy rich who'll whisk me away from all this,' she gestured dramatically with her arm, 'and take me to some warm, idyllic spot—Tahiti, maybe.'

'You wouldn't like Tahiti.' Catherine couldn't help but smile, and it was her first real smile of the entire day. 'It's too hot down there for a woman of your age. Your ankles will start to swell and . . .'

'What do you mean a "woman of my age"—and what's the matter with my ankles?' Maggie lifted her nattily shod foot and looked at her ankle. 'For your information, I'm in my prime. Why, I . . .' The phone suddenly rang in the outer office and she instantly started for the door, the all-efficient secretary was back on the job. 'Are you in—or what?' She glanced back over her shoulder at Catherine.

Catherine's forehead creased into a tired frown. 'No, not for a while, Maggie,' she shook her head. 'I don't feel like talking to anyone right now. If it's somebody who wants to talk to me, take a message. Tell them I'll get back to them later,' she scowled her displeasure at that idea. 'Maybe.'

With the sound of Catherine's office door closing with Maggie's exit, Catherine swirled around in the chair, positioning herself so she could stare out of the window behind her. Maybe Smitty was right—maybe Maggie was right—maybe everybody was right and she should accept the inevitable and call it quits. She let her head droop forward, her chin practically touching her chest as she closed her eyes and gently ran her fingertips across her throbbing temples.

Maggie had had the best idea of them all—Catherine felt a reluctant smile curve her lips—only instead of Maggie finding someone rich to whisk her away to Tahiti, Catherine should be the one doing the looking. But if she knew somebody that rich, she reasoned, she wouldn't have to run away to Tahiti, she could stay right here and run her father's business.

The door to her office opened quietly. 'Catherine?'

'What, Maggie?' Catherine didn't turn around but continued to stare out of the window, her voice sounding slightly muffled from behind the high-backed chair.

'That was Mr Cayhill from the bank on the phone,' Maggie went on to explain, a curious note creeping into her voice. 'He said the strangest thing had just happened.'

'Oh?' It was an anaemic 'oh'—Catherine was beyond caring. What else could happen now? 'I suppose he called to tell me that the bank's computers had fouled up somewhere and made a gigantic mistake in my favour. I don't really owe the bank sixty-three thousand dollars in three days.' Her voice dripped with bitter sarcasm. 'Right?'

'No, that's wrong.' Maggie put her hands on her hips and stared at the back of Catherine's chair. 'And if you'll keep still for two minutes, I'll tell you exactly what he did say.'

Maggie paused and listened, but all was quiet from behind the chair, so she drew a breath and continued. 'He said he'd just had an enquiry from someone interested in Parker Plastics.'

'He did?' This got Catherine's attention in a hurry, and wide-eyed, she spun the chair around to face Maggie. 'What kind of an enquiry was it? What did he say? Did he seem optimistic? This isn't someone interested in a tax loss, is it? Who was it—a firm, a private investor—who? what?' Catherine's face sparkled with renewed life. 'Oh, I knew it would all work out, Maggie!' She clasped her hands together on the top of her desk and laughed with relief. 'All I needed was a little faith—and here you and Smitty were both sounding the death knell and . . .' She finally stopped talking and stared at the sombre stony-faced Maggie. 'Well, don't just stand there, Maggie—say something!'

'I plan on doing that,' Maggie crisped, 'just as soon as you give me the chance to squeeze in two words sideways.'

Catherine laughed. She was feeling too good to be swayed by Maggie's stern looks. 'OK, tell me.'

'I'll tell you.' Maggie paused, her lips pursed in an expression of obvious reluctance. 'And I can tell you everything that needs to be said in only two words. Are you ready for this—Sadler McQuade?'

Catherine's 'high' was an immediate 'low' and her hand fluttered weakly to her stomach as if she had just suffered an unexpected blow. 'Who did you say?' her face paled.

Maggie sighed, 'Sadler Mc . . .'

'Never mind!' Catherine bounced back, shaking her head angrily. 'I heard you perfectly well the first time.' She thinned her lips and narrowed her eyes. 'What has Sadler got to do with any of this?'

'He's the one who approached Mr Cayhill about your note.' Maggie paused warily, looking for the first sign of an explosion from Catherine. 'Mr Cayhill had no idea of Sadler's previous connection with you, of course, but he knew Sadler's name by his reputation.'

'Naturally,' hissed Catherine. 'Who doesn't?'

'. . . and he seemed genuinely relieved that someone was showing an interest in the firm.'

'I'll bet!'

'Of course,' Maggie continued, her voice raising several exasperated tones, 'Mr Cayhill could explain very little. The details and ultimate decision have to come from you.'

Catherine returned Maggie's stare with an even coolness, the tight, narrow expression on her face giving

Maggie no real clue as to what she was thinking. And what she was thinking of was Sadler. Ever since the divorce Catherine had had but one objective in mind, almost to the point of obsession; to forget Sadler McQuade. She had even gone out of her way *not* to mention his name, but yesterday's chance encounter in the restaurant had changed all that and Sadler, or his name, were making themselves obvious with frustrating frequency.

But why now? she mused. Could Parker's be the reason for Sadler's return to Charleston? Catherine answered her own question with a slight shake of her head—that didn't make any sense. But then she always had had a problem trying to figure Sadler out. When they had been married youth and inexperience could have been blamed—she was, after all, only nineteen. But it was more complicated than that, maybe it was more a case of Sadler, at the age of thirty, being just too much of a man for Catherine to handle. Whatever the reason, she would be the first to admit that they had been an explosive couple—able to strike sparks off one another with little or no effort at all.

And it seemed as if nothing had changed in that respect; she still prickled at the thought of him.

'Well, Catherine?' Maggie had evidently waited as long as she could. 'What are you going to do? You wanted a fairy godmother, and this looks like it. What if Sadler *is* willing to bail you out?' Her question was asked in tones of anxious concern. 'What will you do?'

'Bail me out?' Catherine's lips curled with distaste over the expression. 'You make it sound like I'm a charity case! I don't need Sadler's money—or his charity. I've gotten along quite nicely these past few years without him or his money, and I see no reason to change now. There has to be another way to do this, Maggie,' she shook her head firmly, but her voice sounded like an unconscious plea to the gods. 'There *has* to be!'

Maggie's finely plucked eyebrows slowly returned to

their usual form, falling down from the high arc they had obtained with Catherine's claim of getting along quite nicely without Sadler. That was a highly debatable statement, but this certainly wasn't the time to debate it. 'If there's another way you'd better find it—and in a hurry,' Maggie suggested, 'because Sadler's on his way over here now.'

'Thank you, Maggie,' Catherine's voice was flat, dull and unemotional, 'that'll be all. I'll call you if I need you.'

'But what about Sadler?' Maggie watched the big black chair swivel around again, swallowing up Catherine in the process. 'What do you want me to tell him when he gets here?' Her expression hardened. 'Turning your back on him isn't going to solve anything, Catherine. You're going to have to deal with him one way or the other—there's just so much I can do in this situation. You might have gotten away with running out on Sadler once before,' she shook her head slowly, 'but I doubt if you can get away with those tactics again.'

'Thank you, Maggie,' Catherine's voice sharpened noticeably. 'But a marriage is two people, not three. When I want your opinion on my personal life I'll ask for it. I said that was all—shut the door on your way out, please.'

Maggie opened her mouth to reply, but sighed instead and remained still. With a final sympathetic glance in Catherine's direction she quietly closed the door behind as she left.

Looking a lot like a lone, featherless baby chick in its protective nest, Catherine let the chair engulf her while she stared out of the second floor window. Above her a bright blue cloudless sky and below her the black pavement of the company parking lot. It was strange, she thought curiously, how looking now at the nearly empty lot failed to affect her. Maybe it was a case of having had too many drains on her emotions lately for this latest disaster to matter. And seeing Sadler again *was* a disaster—make no mistake about that.

Catherine had no idea what Sadler was driving lately, but she knew intuitively that she would recognise his car when she saw it. When the bright persimmon orange Jaguar rolled to a stop just below her window several minutes later Catherine had no doubt in her mind as to who would step out from behind the wheel.

Like a sleek panther, Sadler McQuade unfurled from the driver's seat of the car and for a moment stood staring up at the building. Secure in her nest, Catherine stared back. From Sadler's position below her it was impossible for him to see into any of the second floor windows, and behind her heavy basket-weave celery-coloured curtains Catherine had the obvious advantage of watching without being watched.

But it was an advantage Catherine didn't want. Tall, dark and more handsome than she remembered, Sadler reached inside his car and removed a narrow brown leather briefcase. The sun caught the gold initials on the top and reflected their blinding beam toward a suddenly breathless Catherine. It was the same briefcase she had given Sadler for their six-month anniversary. Well, why not, she frowned darkly, why shouldn't he still be using it? It was an expensive case, but then Sadler always did demand the very best of everything.

With a growing unease she seemed incapable to squelch. She watched as Sadler fastened the last button on his light tan suit jacket. It was nothing short of incredible, she thought bitterly, that while she'd been going through hell these past few years, Sadler looked exactly the same as he had when they were married. No . . . Catherine shook her head with an honest reluctance for the truth . . . Sadler didn't look the same—he looked better. God, but she had been crazy about him then!

But not now! Angry, Catherine shook her head, sending unwanted memories that were struggling to be recalled, back into a senseless oblivion where they belonged.

'I hate you, Sadler,' Catherine purposely spoke the words out loud, listening with a grim satisfaction as their echo circled the room again and again as she watched him walk towards the entrance and ultimately out of sight. 'I hate you, Sadler McQuade!'

CHAPTER THREE

As Sadler walked across the parking lot, Catherine didn't have to literally 'see' him to know what he was doing. Her mind's eye supplied his every move and she 'watched' him as he walked up to the entrance, opened the doors and stepped inside. A brief glance around to reacquaint himself with the layout of the building, then up the stairs, two at a time, and down the hall to the office of the president.

Almost to the exact second that her mind put Sadler in the outer office, Catherine heard the muffled voices of Maggie and Sadler, Maggie's audible laugh of obvious pleasure at seeing Sadler again only bringing a heavier frown to Catherine's face. Still staring out the window, she took a deep breath and braced herself, waiting for the expected knock to come on the door—and praying that it wouldn't.

'Sadler's here, Catherine,' Maggie announced the news rather soberly from the doorway, her voice trailing off with the barest hint of anxiety. 'Shall I have him come in?' There was no reply coming from the other side of the chair, so Maggie walked closer to the giant desk. 'He looks good, Catherine.' Maggie lowered her voice even though the connecting door to the outer office was closed. 'Even better than I remembered.'

'Who asked you, Maggie?' Catherine snapped off the words. She had already seen Sadler for herself and she didn't need Maggie or anyone else reminding her of how good he looked. 'I'm sorry, Maggie,' she sighed, the sound of her own words leaving a bitter taste in her mouth. 'I didn't mean to snap at you like that, it's just that,' her voice cracked slightly, 'this whole mess has made me slightly crazy. The company—the bank—and now Sadler. I didn't need this, Maggie,' her voice faded, 'I really didn't.'

'I know, Catherine,' Maggie's voice relayed her sympathetic concern. 'But he's here now. You've got to make up your mind what to do—I can't do that for you.' She paused and waited, giving Catherine as much time as she could. 'So what shall I do about Sadler—shall I send him in?'

Catherine, her back still to the door, stared vacantly out the window. Unseen by Maggie, she shrugged, her hands fluttering weakly in a gesture of total helplessness. 'You might as well, Maggie,' Catherine's voice sounded dull and not at all like Catherine. 'I don't suppose that if we kept him waiting long enough he'd finally get the hint and give up, fading off quietly into the sunset. Sadler never did like to wait for anything.' These last few words were whispered, as if they were meant to be a thought, but somehow found their way to her voice.

'Fading off into the sunset isn't my style, Cat,' Sadler's easily recognisable voice came from the now open doorway.' And neither is talking to the back of a chair—so turn around and face me!'

The deep breath that was supposed to help relax her suddenly caught in her throat, making her feel worse instead of better. Bracing herself for what was now the inevitable, she slowly spun her chair around. Dressed in a silk suit of pale apple green with a flurry of mock white ruffles down the front of her jacket and around the cuffs of her sleeves, and sitting in that giant black chair with her hands held limply in her lap, she looked for all the world like the red-haired freckled-nose little girl who used to play office in her daddy's chair.

She had had almost twenty minutes to prepare herself for this meeting with Sadler, and watching him get out of his car had helped—but not enough. Sadler had the type of personality whereby he could walk into a room and every eye was instantly on him. He didn't even have to speak; he was just there and everybody knew it. And

Catherine was no exception.

'Still playing at life, eh, Cat?' Sadler's voice had an unnatural edge to it, his eyes showing a curious displeasure at seeing Catherine in the centre of that huge black chair. 'I think you've missed your true calling—you should have gone on the stage, even though you messed up royally your first role of being the happy little wife. But what is it this time?' His grey eyes narrowed suspiciously. 'Business woman? President of the company? Little girl lost? What?' He waved his hand across the top of her desk. 'I can't tell your role without a programme.'

'Go to hell, Sadler!' Catherine hissed angrily, her cheeks a fiery red. 'I don't know why you're here, but if it's simply to do a belated post-mortem on the worst eight months of my entire life, then you can forget it. Like anything that dies, Sadler,' her green eyes snapped, 'you bury it and let it rest in peace, and our marriage—such as it was—is long since dead.'

'Ah,' he drawled, an unpleasant smile accompanying the sound, 'but there's the catch. Our marriage didn't merely die, Cat. You killed it—choked the life right out of it—and like anything that loses its life due to *murder*,' he leaned forward over her desk and lowered his voice to a theatrical whisper. 'Its ghost lingers on to haunt us even now.'

'Maggie?' Catherine said slowly, ignoring Sadler and looking past him towards the older woman who was in the process of backing her way unnoticed towards the open doorway. 'Maggie . . .' she repeated, purely for effect. 'Get in touch with security and have them throw this,' her eyes narrowed as she finally looked at Sadler, 'this *person* out. If he refuses to leave call the police and have him arrested for trespassing.'

'Catherine!' Maggie was appalled by Catherine's suggestion and her eyes widened with alarm. This was a bit drastic, even for Catherine, because not only was the order a little wild—it was also impossible to carry out.

They didn't have any security. 'Sadler, I . . .' Words failed her, and she shrugged apologetically at Sadler.

But Sadler didn't look the least bit upset—he was far from it, and his easy smile was meant to put her at ease. 'Don't look so upset, Maggie,' he tried to reassure her. 'We'll just chalk that up to some of Cat's wild ravings. In a minute or two she'll get it all out of her system and settle down so we can get on with our business. That's all for now, Maggie,' he smiled again, knowing how anxious she was to leave. 'If we need anything I'll call you.'

'*Don't take one more step, Maggie!*' Catherine immediately countermanded Sadler's orders, so furious with him that she stammered half the words just getting them out. 'Just who in the hell do you think you are!' she glared at him. 'Waltzing in here and giving orders to *my staff*! I think you're a little confused, Sadler,' she added tightly. 'This is my place of business, not yours.'

Surprisingly, Sadler's expression was immediately repentant, not the response she would have anticipated, and her eyes narrowed warily. 'You're absolutely right,' he purred silkily. 'I was jumping the gun—a little. I apologise. You're still in charge,' he paused, '—for now.'

Sadler never was one for subtleties and his meaning came across loud and clear. He *was* here with the obvious intention of taking over Parker Plastics—or trying to, Catherine amended silently. Their eyes met, and as Catherine watched the premature smile of victory form behind a curtain of smoky grey she made up her mind. No matter what kind of deal or proposition Sadler had in mind, her answer was going to be no. She'd let her father's business go bankrupt before she'd accept one thin dime of help from Sadler!

With her decision made and firm in her mind, Catherine could afford to relax a little and be polite, if not friendly. There was nothing Sadler could do now to change her mind. Smiling sweetly, she turned to Maggie, still frozen on the spot. 'It's all right, Maggie, you can go. We won't be needing you, unless . . .' she turned her brilliant smile towards Sadler, 'could I have Maggie bring you something, Sadler? Coffee perhaps, or tea? I'm afraid we don't have anything stronger.'

It was Sadler's turn to look wary—and he did. 'No, thank you, Cat,' he shook his head, his grey eyes narrowing.

'Oh? Pity.' Catherine looked like the perfect hostess who had just spent hours in the kitchen preparing a gourmet's delight and now no one wanted any. 'I guess that's all, then, Maggie,' she shrugged. 'You may go—thank you.'

While Maggie made a hasty retreat, Sadler sat down in the chair opposite Catherine and slid his briefcase across the top of the desk between them. For a moment all he did was stare at her. 'You surprise me, Cat,' he admitted softly, the tiny lines at the corners of his eyes deepening. 'I expected you to throw a tantrum and that part about having security throw me out was good, but this . . .' he waved his hand across the top of her desk, 'this calm, sweet-smiling Cheshire Cat isn't you.'

He sat back in his chair and conducted a very thorough but impartial assessment of the woman in front of him. 'Maybe I was wrong yesterday in the restaurant,' he admitted tentatively. 'You have changed. I think it's quite possible that the past few years have added a little maturity to you after all.'

'Why, thank you, Sadler,' Catherine's pale rose lips curved into a warm, perfect smile, but her eyes betrayed her—they were still cold as green ice. 'That's quite generous a statement for you to make—to finally admit that I've grown up.'

'Oh, but I didn't say that,' he suddenly laughed. 'You've grown older, who hasn't, but I haven't seen much evidence that you've grown up. There's a big difference, Cat.'

Catherine clung to the arms of her chair and what was

left of her failing good humour. 'That's only your opinion, Sadler.' It was getting harder for her to smile. 'And since you haven't been around to see any changes in me, I don't think your opinion in this case matters in the least—not to me it doesn't.'

'Ah, that's better,' he smiled, and nodded comfortably. 'Now you're beginning to sound like the Cat I knew and loved—in one of my more insane moments. Cat . . .' he repeated her name with a slow smile, 'Cat never was a fond diminutive form of Catherine, did you know that?' He waited, but she didn't answer him, so he shrugged and continued, 'I called you Cat not because of your name, but because of your actions. Whenever you found yourself pushed into a corner, your back would go up and you'd spring to the attack. That's a pretty good tactic,' he admitted, 'and I've used it myself, but it's not going to work this time—not with me.'

'No? Then what will work with you, Sadler?' Catherine asked dryly. 'You tell me—what do I have to do to get rid of you? Throw you out of here myself?'

'Now there's an interesting idea.' He lowered his dark, thick lashes and peered at her as if he was actually considering it. 'But I wouldn't go without putting up a fight. Do you want to risk that, Cat?' His voice softened to a lazy purr, the look in his eyes purposely warm and seductive. 'Do you want to risk all that touching and being close?' The look in his eyes intensified. 'Or is all that a thing of the past?'

Catherine knew what he was referring to and there was nothing she could do to prevent her cheeks from burning. Out of all the hundreds of things that had gone wrong in their marriage, making love wasn't one of them. And Sadler, as a lover, was a master at getting what he wanted, and it invariably started with a touch.

She shook her head angrily. 'Again you flatter yourself, Sadler. I wouldn't touch you with a bargepole, but I don't have to,' she sneered, the hot red spots on her cheeks finally beginning to fade. 'I have employees hired to do just that.'

'You mean your security?' He started to laugh, then stopped, his expression changing as he leaned across the top of her desk, his face only inches from hers. 'You don't have security of any kind. What you do have, my dear Cat,' his voice lowered dramatically, 'is a company about to go down the tubes. Your financial statement for the last fiscal year was a joke. In your case I think it should have been called "loss and loss" instead of "profit and loss". There was so much red ink I had to read it with sunglasses on just to keep from blinding myself.'

'How dare you!' Catherine jumped to her feet, her hands slapping angrily on the top of her desk. 'You had no business . . .'

'No!' he interrupted, cutting her off with an angry shake of his head. 'You're the one who has no business, or soon won't have. What I have is sixty-three thousand dollars that I'm willing to spend in order to save your skin. In return for bailing you out I want . . .'

'No!' Catherine didn't care what he wanted—he wasn't going to get it.

'In return,' he repeated firmer and louder, 'I want total controlling interest in the firm. And that's not just financial control,' he explained, shaking his head emphatically to make his point. 'I want a hand in the day-to-day management. No . . .' he pursed his lips thoughtfully, 'not just a hand. I want it *all*. The right to hire and fire at will, the right to make all the decisions *without your interference*, the right . . .'

'*No!*' Catherine was almost beside herself with rage.

'. . . and,' he continued, 'the right to do what I see fit with any and all of the company assets—such as they are.' Having dropped his little bombshell, Sadler sat back in his chair and waited, his grey eyes never wavering from her face.

'You can't be serious,' she whispered hoarsely, her throat so dry it hurt her to talk.

'Oh, but I am, Cat,' Sadler's eyes darkened, 'I'm totally serious.'

'Do you know what that'll leave me?' her voice cracked with tears and emotion. 'Nothing! Not a damn thing. I've been running this business for three years, and in spite of the difficulties it's in now, I've done a darn good job. If I do what you want me to,' she paused; it was beginning to hurt her to breathe, 'you'll own the company.'

'That's about it,' he nodded his dark head easily in agreement.

'And you think that I'm going to roll over and play dead and hand over to you everything my father and I worked for?' Catherine's hands trembled so badly she had to clutch them together tightly in her lap to keep from shaking all over. 'If you do, you've got another thing coming, because I'm not going to do that—ever!'

Infuriatingly calm and still relaxed, Sadler opened his briefcase and idly thumbed through the top few sheets of papers. 'When's the last time Maggie had a full week's salary?'

'What?' Caught unprepared by Sadler's question, Catherine blanched. She naïvely thought that all Sadler's little surprises were over, but she should have known better then that—he always saved the best for the end. He was guessing—she narrowed her eyes hopefully. How could he possibly know that Maggie had been accepting partial salary for nearly two months now—and poor Smitty, she thought wretchedly, it had been even longer then that for him.

'And what about yourself?' Sadler continued unrelentingly, snapping out his questions like a prosecuting attorney. 'When's the last time you drew *any* of your salary? Outside of taking the barest living expenses you haven't had a full week's pay since . . .' he paused and glanced at his papers, inadvertently giving Catherine a chance for rebuttal.

And she jumped at it. 'What I do or don't do, Sadler,'

she snapped before he had the chance to continue, 'is none of your business. In fact,' she waved her hand irritably, '*none* of this is any of your business because we don't have a deal—and never will. So why don't you pick up your little papers and trot yourself . . .'

'Oh, but I think we do have a deal,' he countered smoothly, Catherine's outburst not affecting him at all. 'In fact, I'm certain of it. I understand that the bank has given you three days to come up with the money. I'm giving you *two* days to make up your mind, although,' he paused lazily, 'I don't see where there's anything *to* consider. Look around you, Cat,' he waved his hand. 'Your employees have been slowly deserting the ship. The few that are left are either like Maggie—loyal—or else they're too old to find a new job easily. They should be getting ready to retire, not thinking about starting a whole new career. So before you say no simply out of pique, stop and give some thought to them.'

Catherine's face went as white as a sheet. There wasn't a day that went by without her thinking about them. 'You bastard!' she hissed through her teeth. 'That's all I have been thinking about!'

'Forty-eight hours, Cat,' he replied, a muscle tensing visibly alongside his jaw. 'No more. Time's run out for you.' He stood up and snapped his briefcase closed with an echo of finality that seemed to hang like a shroud on Catherine's shoulders. He turned and started for the door.

'Oh?' He snapped his fingers and smiled faintly in her direction. 'I almost forgot to tell you—I ran into your friend Sophia at the bank this afternoon. I didn't realise she was Mr Cayhill's secretary. We had a very nice chat—she said to tell you hello.'

'Did she? I'll bet that made her whole day,' Catherine returned sourly, remembering the look on Sophia's face when she first met Sadler in the restaurant.

'What did?'

'Why, running into you again, Sadler,' she replied

coolly. 'What else? She must have been ecstatic.'

'But of course she was, my dear Cat,' he laughed softly. 'I'm having dinner with her this evening.'

'Who cares?' Catherine let her lip curl with obvious displeasure.

'You do, Cat,' Sadler's smile vanished just that quickly, 'you do. Forty-eight hours,' he warned her. 'I'll call you.'

Emotionally drained and physically exhausted, Catherine crumbled up like the last dry leaf of autumn and collapsed into her father's chair. It seemed impossible to believe that after all these years he could still do it to her—he could walk into a room and she'd feel everything all over again; the physical desire, the loathing, the tears.

What was the matter with her? Angry, frustrated and unable to answer her own question, she began to laugh, softly at first, then a little louder.

'Catherine?' Maggie had already started into the office when she heard Catherine begin to laugh. 'What did Sadler say to . . .' She stopped—the look on Catherine's face didn't go with the sound of laughter. 'That's enough, Catherine. Stop it!' Only Catherine couldn't stop it and Maggie had to shake her—hard enough to make her head snap back and forth. 'Stop it!' Maggie shouted at her. 'Do you hear me? I said that's enough!'

With a final few sobs that sounded more like a whimper then a sob, Catherine stopped laughing and slowly began to cry. 'Oh, Maggie,' she sobbed, her eyes filling rapidly with tears, 'Sadler was the only man I ever met who could make cry and look at me—he's *still* the only man who can make me cry. Why? Why do I let him get to me like this?'

'I don't know, Catherine.' Maggie stood back and looked at her, Catherine's crying a healthy release and not the worrisome touch of near hysteria. 'I suppose it's because both of you have dominating personalities and every time you get together you burn up all your energy fighting him. When you do that you can't keep anything in reserve to protect yourself.'

She sighed sympathetically and sat down in the chair Sadler had just vacated. 'What is it this time?'

'That sounds like you think it's *my* fault that I'm upset.' Catherine reached in her desk drawer for a tissue, wiped her eyes and sat back in her chair.

'And isn't it?' Maggie probed gently.

'No, not this time.' Catherine took a moment to wipe away a sniffle before she continued. 'Maybe you're right about my using up all my energy fighting Sadler, but I've got good cause. Sadler's like . . .' she paused thoughtfully, 'like some huge ball of energy that feeds itself on other people's energy. When he drains them of everything they've got he just spits them out like so much trash.'

'I assume that what you're talking about now is the reason for Sadler's visit today.' Maggie frowned—she wasn't sure. 'Parker Plastics and the bank?'

'Of course that's what I'm talking about.' Catherine looked surprised that Maggie could have got any other impression. 'Sadler,' her voice tightened, 'in his infinite generosity, has made me a deal.' This brought a bitter smile to her still pale lips. 'He's willing to "save my skin", as he so eloquently put it, by paying off the note at the bank.'

'Really? All of it?' Maggie looked encouraged. 'That sounds like a good . . .'

'Let me finish first,' Catherine interrupted quickly, 'and then you can tell me what you think. Like I said,' she subconsciously squared her shoulders as if the mere thought of Sadler made her brace herself. 'Sadler will pay off in toto the loan at the bank. In return for which all he wants is . . .' she paused for dramatic effect, '*everything!* Lock, stock and barrel,' her eyes widened. 'He wants it all—complete control of Parker Plastics—management as well as financial. I'm not to have any say-so in how things are done from now on.'

'Well?' she exclaimed smugly. 'Now what do you think of Sadler's kind, generous offer now?'

'I think,' Maggie looked a little uncomfortable as she tried to answer Catherine's question, 'that you don't have any choice. No matter what Sadler's terms are you're going to have to accept them. *If* you want to save Parker Plastics, that is.'

'Maggie!'

'You asked for my opinion this time, Catherine,' Maggie shook her head and shrugged. 'I can't help it if that's not what you wanted to hear, but that's it—that's my opinion.'

'You and Smitty always did like Sadler!' Catherine made it sound like a vile accusation.

'Yes, I suppose we did,' Maggie agreed easily. 'Smitty knows Sadler better than I do, but that's really not the point and had nothing to do with this. On a purely business level, I don't see where you've got a choice. It's not as if you've had dozens of offers where you can pick and choose the deal you like best. Face it, Catherine,' Maggie's expression hardened, 'it's Sadler McQuade or nothing.'

'Then it's nothing, Maggie,' Catherine's reply was soft but firm. 'Sadler's price is too high. I can't afford to let him back into my life again—not after what it cost me emotionally to get rid of him the first time. Not again,' her vow was a whisper. 'Never again.'

Smitty held the front door to the apartment open and stepped to one side, smiling sympathetically at Catherine as she dragged herself inside. 'I'm not even going to bother to ask you how it went with Mr Cayhill today—' Smitty paused, 'because I already know. Maggie called me.'

'Did she?' Catherine's slim shoulders drooped indifferently. 'I'm not surprised. I suppose she told you all about Sadler, too?'

'She did,' Smitty nodded, unaffected by the sudden sharpness in Catherine's voice. 'And you're not going to like this, but I have to say I agree with her. Money's money, Catherine,' he followed her into the living-room. 'What difference does it make where it comes from?'

'A lot!' Catherine made a sour face as she sat down on the sofa. 'It's not the money, per se,' she waved her hand absently, 'it's all the strings attached to it. Sadler's not merely content to buy into Parker Plastics as an investment, he wants it all—and he wants it handed to him on a silver platter. If I agree to Sadler's demands, Smitty,' Catherine sighed, 'he'll end up with everything but my soul.' She thinned her lips and stared vacantly into space. 'And I'm certain that if he could figure out a way to get *that*, he would, too.' Sadler was a depressing subject and Catherine ran her fingers tiredly through her hair, seeking at least a momentary respite. 'How about something cold to drink?'

'Coming right up,' Smitty nodded. 'What would you like?'

Catherine closed her eyes and shook her head. 'I don't know—you decide for me. Surprise me. After the day I've had I don't want to do anything any more cerebral than deciding if I want to eat my peas ahead of my mashed potatoes.'

'I made some fresh lemonade today,' Smitty decided with a worried frown. 'I'll get you a glass of that. You know, Catherine,' his voice floated back to her from the kitchen, 'I'm beginning to think this is all getting too much for you. Why don't you forget it and get away for a while?'

'Don't I wish!' She reached up for the tall glass of cold lemonade. 'Thanks. But I can't leave, Smitty—not now. I've only got a few days to come up with the solution. *Me*,' she tapped her chest, 'nobody else. Whether I like it or not I'm the only one who can decide what to do. And as Sadler was so eager to point out to me today,' her eyes hardened, 'I've got a lot of people depending on me to do something—the *right* something.'

'Well then,' Smitty gestured, the solution seemed obvious to him, 'take Sadler's offer.'

'I can't do that, Smitty.' Catherine's chin drooped lightly. 'This is one case where the cure will *definitely* be worse then the disease!'

'So . . .' his lips thinned, 'you're willing to let Parker's go bankrupt.'

It was a sickening thought, and Catherine's expression reflected exactly that. 'If it comes right down to it—yes. But there has to be some way to raise that much money *without* going to Sadler for it.'

'I haven't mentioned this before,' Smitty cleared his throat hoarsely, 'but I've managed to save a little something over the years. You know,' he shrugged, 'something for a rainy day. It's not much, Catherine, but it's yours if you want it.'

'Oh, Smitty,' Catherine got a catch in her throat, 'that's sweet of you, really it is.' Her eyes filled with tears. 'But you'd better hang on to it. The way things are going it looks like *you* might end up supporting *me*.'

She quickly wiped off the tears before they could spill visibly down her cheeks, a teasing new thought bringing a small smile to her lips. 'And that brings up an interesting point,' she paused, letting her eyes widen slowly. 'How could you possibly have saved anything on what I've been paying you—or not paying you, as the case may be. Have you been dipping your beak into the household fund?'

'Certainly!' he agreed with a broad grin. 'How else was I going to obtain complete financial independence without working for it?'

'Oh, Smitty!' Tears began to flow again and disgusted with her emotional state Catherine forcibly swiped at the offending tears. 'Look at me!' she ordered, holding up her hand for inspection—it was trembling. 'I'm a basket case—bawling like some silly schoolgirl. I haven't cried in years, and Sadler's back in town for ten minutes and I can't seem to *stop* crying!'

'Crying's not so bad, Catherine,' Smitty gave her a much needed affectionate hug. 'The trick is to realise exactly what it is you're crying for.' He sat down next to her on the sofa, handing her his handkerchief as he did. 'Here, blow your nose. Did I tell you Maggie's coming for dinner?'

'No,' she sniffled and tried to smile, 'you didn't. That's great.' She paused. 'Smitty?'

'What, Catherine?'

'When are you going to marry Maggie?' It was a question she had had on her mind a lot lately and she waited solemnly for Smitty to reply.

'My, my!' he cocked a greying eyebrow. 'Aren't we nosey? Don't you have enough to worry about without playing matchmaker as well?'

Catherine dismissed his reply with a soft scowl. 'Maggie's in love with you.'

'I know that,' he nodded.

'Well then!' her green eyes came to life. 'Do something about it—marry her! That's generally what's supposed to happen when two people love one another.'

'It's not the right time, Catherine,' Smitty's voice sounded strained and his face had a look about it that she didn't understand.

'Not the right time?' she echoed weakly. 'What time does it have to be? Smitty . . . *darling* . . .' she drawled, hanging on to his hand, 'neither one of you is getting any younger.'

'Thank you,' he replied dryly. 'But our rapidly advancing ages aren't the problem.'

'Then what is?' Catherine asked; she really wanted to know. If the reason that the two favourite people in her life weren't getting married was the problem at Parker Plastics . . . that would be too much to take on top of everything else. 'If you and Maggie got married,' she pointed out hopefully, 'then I wouldn't have to worry about you.'

'You mean if Parker's folds?'

Catherine didn't answer him, but she didn't have to. Smitty knew. 'So why don't you marry Maggie?' The softness of her voice begged for an answer.

Smitty drew a deep breath before he replied, taking his time and searching for just the right words. 'Maggie's been married before—you know that—and she had a good marriage, right up to the time when her husband died. As far as I'm concerned, I'd marry her tomorrow and I've told her so. But I'm only half—the rest is up to her, and I can't rush her. She's got to feel right about it in her own mind, and until she does all I can do is wait.' He cocked an eyebrow. 'See?'

'I guess so,' Catherine shrugged—then changed her mind. 'No, I don't see. What is she waiting for? It's so unnecessary—especially when both of you feel exactly the same way about one another. When two people love one another they should . . .'

'Hello. Where is everybody?' Maggie's voice came from the kitchen. 'I came in the back door expecting to find busy hands preparing food. My mouth was already beginning to water,' she stopped and grinned at them from the living-room doorway, 'and what do I find?—I find the two of you in here . . .' her eyes spotted the glass in Catherine's hand. 'Doing what—drinking?'

'Only lemonade,' Catherine laughed, and held up her glass. 'Smitty and I got to talking about . . . well, one thing and the other, and we didn't notice the time.' She got to her feet. 'As long as you're here you can keep Smitty company while I shower and change. If I could,' she adding, frowning to no one in particular, 'I'd like to wash this whole day from my mind.'

When she was halfway down the hallway towards her bedroom, the phone rang, bringing her to a temporary halt. 'Somebody get that, will you?' she waved her hand absently and kept walking. 'If it's for me I don't want to talk to anybody. I just want to relax tonight and take it easy.'

Once inside her bedroom Catherine prepared for a shower, stepping out of her apple green suit and into an ankle-length, clinging white robe, slit thigh-high front and back. Fastening it loosely around her waist, she started towards the bathroom off her bedroom.

'Catherine?' Maggie's voice from the other side of the bedroom door was accompanied by a few sharp raps with her knuckles. 'Smitty told me to tell you Sadler's on the phone!'

Catherine froze, her hand on the bathroom doorknob, her eyes going instantly to the pink phone next to her bed. 'Tell him I'm not home yet,' she called her instructions back to Maggie while her green eyes intently watched the phone—almost as if she expected Sadler to suddenly jump out of it. 'I don't want to talk to him.'

'I can't do that.' Maggie opened the door and stepped in. 'Smitty's already told him you were home,' she shrugged apologetically.

'OK, so tell him I'm in the shower. Two more minutes and I will be. Or,' Catherine smiled tightly, 'if you want to, tell him the truth. Tell him I don't want to talk to him.'

Maggie drew a long deep sigh. 'You don't really think that's going to work, do you? The best you could hope to do would be to stall him for a few minutes. He'll only call back and keep on calling back until you talk to him. You know better than I do how Sadler gets when he's determined. You might as well talk to him now and get it over with,' she shrugged. 'Besides, he said it was important.'

Catherine *did* know Sadler, and muttering under her breath, she marched across to the phone. 'All right,' she snapped irritably at Maggie. 'But this is going to be quick.' With an angry gesture she snatched up the receiver. 'What do you want, Sadler?'

'Don't you say "hello" first?' his masculine voice enquired softly with surprise.

'No,' Catherine answered quickly, pursing her lips. 'You told Smitty it was important, so get on with it. What is it—what do you want?'

'It is important, Cat,' he replied stiffly, the softness gone from his voice. 'We need to get together and discuss a few things—tonight.'

'We did all our discussing this afternoon, Sadler,' she reminded him impatiently. 'Or have you forgotten already?'

'No, Cat, I haven't forgotten,' he replied. 'But this is in connection with that talk.'

'I haven't changed my mind, Sadler, if that's what you wanted to know. And I'm not going to.' Catherine's grip tightened on the phone. 'So you can stop calling me every two minutes to harass me. In fact,' she paused, 'you can stop calling me—period. Goodbye, Sadler.'

'Don't you *dare* hang up on me, Catherine,' he warned her quietly but firmly, 'or you'll be sorry. And that's not an idle threat, Cat. You know me well enough for that.'

Her hand wavered in mid-air as she struggled to decide whether to disregard his warning or not. She could almost imagine the superior look on his face right now, and wouldn't she just love to hang up on him *and* his warning! Her mouth drooped and reluctantly she returned the phone to her ear. He was still talking to her.

'Are you there, Cat?' he snapped. 'Answer me, damn it! If you've hung up . . .'

'I'm still here, Sadler,' she hissed through her teeth. 'What is it that you want?'

When he heard her voice he drew a long, deep breath. 'I didn't want to get into all this on the phone, Cat,' he paused, 'but your attitude leaves me no alternative. After I left your office this afternoon,' he continued, 'I went back to the bank and saw . . .'

'Really, Sadler,' Catherine drawled in bored tones, 'I don't know what you classify as important, but I'm not the least bit interested in hearing about the sordid details of your tacky little affairs.'

'What the hell are you talking about?' The level of Sadler's voice was as close to a shout as it could be. It was only with the greatest control on his part that it wasn't.

'Sophia,' Catherine answered, somewhat surprised by his reaction. 'You took great delight in telling me about your date with her this evening. Isn't that why you're calling now to . . .'

'Hardlyyouidiot!' Sadler was so furious with her that he ran the three words all together. 'Catherine . . .' he paused, struggling to hold on to what was left of his temper, 'I don't know what there is about you, but you have the uncanny ability to drive me up the wall like no one else I've ever known!'

His comment certainly wasn't intended to be a compliment, but Catherine's smile indicated she accepted it as one. 'Tsk, tsk,' she smirked noisily. 'Isn't that a real shame!'

'Cat,' he groaned, 'if you'll only shut up for one minute I'll come to the point and we can terminate this conversation.'

'Oh, all right, Sadler,' Catherine agreed. He did have a point—and as much fun as this was, she was beginning to get bored with it all. 'But get on with it, will you? I'm busy.'

'Gladly.' He paused only briefly and when he continued his voice was an icy calm which *should* have been Catherine's first hint. 'I went back to the bank after our meeting today,' he repeated, 'and I bought up your note. As of four-fifteen this afternoon, you owe me sixty-three thousand dollars, plus an added amount of interest. I've decided against either extending the time or calling the note immediately—so as far as you're concerned the terms are the same. In three days either I get the money or I foreclose on Parker's.' The line seemed dead to Sadler, so he paused and listened. 'Cat? Are you still there? Did you hear what I just said?'

Catherine had heard every one of his words. The trouble was she couldn't believe them. Her face pale, she swallowed hard, her voice a weak whisper. 'What did you say?' She fought to the end against accepting the reality of what she had just heard.

'I said,' he replied coolly, 'that I bought up your note. This afternoon at approximately four-fifteen I became, to all intents and purposes, the new owner of Parker Plastics.'

'You can't do that!' She still refused to believe him.

'But I just did,' he assured her mercilessly.

'You told me I could think about it,' she reminded him desperately. A moment ago she had had absolutely no intention of letting Sadler finesse his way into Parker Plastics—but that was a moment ago. 'You told me I had forty-eight hours to make up my mind.'

'Well, I changed my mind since then,' he replied, and Catherine could almost hear him shrug. 'After our little chat today,' he continued, 'I had this funny feeling that in forty-eight hours your answer would be exactly the same as it was this afternoon. I couldn't wait and take the chance that you'd let Parker's wind up as a bad debt for the bank simply out of pure spite.' He paused. 'Now do you agree that it's important we discuss this . . . tonight?'

She was in shock. 'Yes,' she whispered weakly into the phone.

'What?' Sadler demanded. He had the upper hand and he wasn't going to let her forget it. 'I didn't hear your answer, Cat. What did you say?'

'I said *yes*, damn it!' she shouted.

'Fine.' She could hear the smug smile in his voice. 'I'll be there in about twenty minutes.'

CHAPTER FOUR

'HE can't do that to me!' Eyes blazing, cheeks a livid red, Catherine slammed her bedroom door and marched down the hallway towards the living-room where Smitty and Maggie were waiting for her. 'That man!' She was so furious she could barely unclench her teeth long enough to speak. 'Only this afternoon he told me I had forty-eight hours to make up my mind—didn't he, Maggie?' But before Maggie could open her mouth to agree Catherine was off again, this time pacing back and forth to keep up with her avalanche of thoughts—none of them very nice.

'Of all the sneaky, underhanded dirty tricks that anybody could pull,' she gestured wildly above her head, 'Sadler's certainly scraped the bottom of the barrel this time! And his excuse—can you believe this?' she rolled her eyes, '—is to claim he did it because he knew I was going to say no and there wasn't any sense in waiting till the last minute. How did he know I was going to say no? And even if I *was* going to tell him no, he still owed it to me to give me the two days like he promised.

'That's typical Sadler, though,' her lips curled with self-reproach. 'I should have remembered how he says one thing and then does something else. How could I be stupid enough to believe he'd do anything on the up-and-up, when I know what a two-faced sneak he really is?'

She suddenly spun around and wagged an accusing finger at Smitty, as if this was somehow his fault. 'And don't tell me he wasn't playing slap and tickle with that politico's dark-eyed daughter in Argentina either, because I know better.' Her expression was one of open contempt, 'Her with her long black hair and dark eyes, and *nobody* walks that way naturally! All that sashaying and . . .'

'You've lost me, Catherine.' Smitty took a chance and plunged in while Catherine was slowing down to take a much-needed breath. 'I thought we were talking about Sadler in relation to your note. How did we get off on the subject of Argentina and your marriage?' He paused, his expression stiffening slightly. 'But as you've brought it up, Catherine, I never believed for a minute that Sadler was involved with her or anyone else. And I know what you're going to say,' his hand came up to stop her, 'you're going to tell me that I wasn't there—I know that, but you've never said anything to convince me that Sadler was unfaithful either. So why don't you just forget all that and tell us what he wanted on the phone?'

'But that's what I was doing.' Catherine stopped her nervous pacing and stared at him.

'Not exactly, Catherine,' Smitty shook his head, his voice softening with compassion. 'What you were doing was dredging up something that did or didn't happen years ago and has no connection with the problem at hand.'

'Well, I . . .' Catherine was at a loss for words. Why *had* she brought all that up now? 'I . . . er . . . I was using it only as an example of Sadler's duplicity. But I think I've made my point.' She paused and cleared her throat; some of her reply had evidently stuck around the edges. 'Well?'

'Well what?'

With an expression of mild annoyance on her face, Catherine glanced questioningly from Smitty to Maggie and back. 'Well, what do you think I should do about Sadler's latest dirty trick?'

Smitty's expression mirrored exactly the totally blank look on Maggie's face. 'We might be able to give you an intelligent response, honey,' he shrugged his shoulder and smiled, 'if we knew what Sadler's latest dirty trick was. What's he done now?'

'Oh,' Catherine looked stunned, 'I haven't told you?' Maggie and Smitty both shook their heads no. 'Well,' a raised eyebrow showed Catherine's instant displeasure, 'after he came to see me this afternoon and told me I had forty-eight hours to make up my mind and accept his generous offer—a foregone conclusion *he* thought—the sneak turned right around and went back to Mr Cayhill and bought up my note! Naturally,' her lips thinned, 'he's not going to make it easy for me by extending the deadline, so now I've got to come up with the money to pay him, instead of the bank.'

'And to make matters worse,' Catherine continued with a loud groan, 'if that's even possible—he's on his way over here now to talk about it. *Gloat* over it would probably be a better description!'

She sagged and collapsed into the nearest chair, her fingers gently massaging her throbbing temples. 'This is just a nightmare,' she whispered, her eyelids closed. 'It has to be. In a little while I'll wake up and all this will be just something I ate.'

'Fine,' Maggie nodded. 'But while we're waiting for you to wake up, might I suggest you put some clothes on? That's a beautiful robe, Catherine, and absolutely perfect for a seduction, but I think it's a little impractical for a serious business discussion.'

Catherine glanced down, surprised to see that the slit in her robe had exposed a good deal of shapely leg. 'Oh! You're right,' she gasped, and jumped to her feet. 'I'm going to have a cool, clear head if I'm going to have any chance of talking him into extending the deadline, or making *some* kind of an arrangement,' she added with a half-hearted sigh. 'How about a nice pin-stripe three-piece suit? Business is business and . . .' Halfway out of the living-room and headed towards her bedroom, she stopped suddenly, spinning around to face Maggie. 'What did you say?' she demanded, her eyes wide and flashing green specks of brilliant light.

'Nothing.' Maggie shook her head with surprise. 'I

didn't say anything, Catherine. You were the one doing all the talking.'

'No, no, not now—before.' Catherine put a mysterious Mona Lisa smile on her face as she glanced down at herself, the clinging bodice and provocative slit in her robe bringing a strange gleam to her eyes. 'Didn't you say something about being dressed for a seduction and not a business meeting? On second thoughts,' her smile widened, 'I don't think I'll change after all.'

Catherine's look of smugness was countered by Smitty's expression of instant and overwhelming displeasure. 'I hope I'm not following your line of thought, Catherine,' his voice sounded strangely subdued, 'but if I am I have only word of advice—don't. You'll only make matters worse.' He was being prophetic and didn't know it. 'This is business,' he continued, 'so treat it as such. And besides,' he shrugged, 'it won't work. Sadler will see through that ploy the moment he steps inside the apartment and gets his first good look of you parading around here half naked.'

'Not necessarily.' Catherine's eyes sparkled like rare champagne with tiny bubbles of one-upmanship fermenting behind the green. 'He doesn't have to know it's planned. I'm certainly not going to be draped all over the sofa when he comes in. I'm not going to be *that* obvious, Smitty!' She paused for a moment and looked thoughtful, her plan gaining more momentum with every passing second. 'When I answer the door I'll just tell him he's early and explain that I'd hoped to take a quick shower before he got here.' Her eyes widened with innocence. 'That's possible.'

'It's not bad,' Smitty reluctantly admitted. 'But I think I can see a small flaw in your plan. Why are you answering the door? *You* should be in the shower and one of us should be answering the door.'

It took only a second for Catherine to puzzle that out. 'But that's impossible, my dear Smitty,' she smiled slowly, 'because you're not going to be here to answer the door. In fact,' she glanced anxiously towards the wall clock, 'you're late as it is.'

'We are?' Practically silent up to now, Maggie finally spoke, her finely plucked brows arching sharply. 'Late for what?'

'For dinner,' Catherine explained impatiently, 'or a show, or anything you and Smitty want. I don't care—just as long as you're not here.'

'Uh-huh!' Smitty smiled, and shook his head no, planting his feet squarely on the floor, 'we're not moving an inch out of this apartment. I'm not leaving you here to carry out a crazy scheme like that.'

'But you've got to . . . *please!*' Catherine was reduced to pleading, time was running out. 'This could very well be my only chance. I can't come up with the money and we all know it, including Sadler. But maybe if I play my cards right I can convince him to . . .'

'Do you know what you're saying?' Maggie looked like a woman on the verge of collapse. 'Do you know what they call women who sell themselves for money or favours?'

Catherine blanched—but only momentarily. She hadn't thought of what she was doing in quite those terms. 'Sure I do,' she nodded, 'but look at it this way, Maggie—' she paused, peering at Maggie through her lashes. Maggie was a lamb, but she had a tendency to be just a trifle stuffy. 'For sixty-three thousand dollars it's bound to be the most expensive one in history. Well,' she frowned lightly, 'maybe not, but right up there among the top ten.'

Catherine saw the resulting look on their faces and started to laugh. 'Relax, will you! I haven't the slightest intention of going through with anything like that. Sadler's not the only one who can play dirty,' her expression hardened. 'I can change my mind at the last minute, too. It happens all the time.'

'It's not going to work,' repeated Smitty, drawing a long breath and letting it out slowly. 'Not with Sadler,

Catherine,' he shook his head.

'Sure it is.' Catherine was more determined than ever. 'And it will work because it *is* Sadler. Don't forget I was married to him and I know him—*well*. All I have to do is distract him,' she gnawed a little nervously on her lower lip—this was the tricky part in her plan. 'At least long enough to get him to agree to a deal that's in my favour, not his.'

'You didn't learn anything being married to Sadler, did you?' Smitty shook his had sadly. 'He was too much for you to handle then, what makes you think now is going to be any different?'

'I was too young when we were married,' Catherine replied tightly, 'I'll admit that, but I'm older now.'

'Older maybe, but no wiser,' Smitty replied, unknowingly echoing Sadler's own words. 'At least not when it comes to Sadler. He's shrewd, Catherine, and always has been. That's why he's gotten as far as he has.'

'For the sake of argument,' Maggie chimed in with a little flip of her hand, 'let's say Sadler goes along with your scheme, but demands a little show of faith from you and not just empty promises. In short, Catherine, what's going to happen when he makes you put your money where your mouth is? Although,' she frowned lightly, 'it isn't your money you're offering, is it? Under those circumstances I don't think a cry of rape will hold up in court.'

'He wouldn't dare!'

'How can you be so sure?' Maggie's staid expression grew expressive. 'If you start making wild promises, Sadler's just the man to make certain you keep them.'

'Ah, but that's just it,' Catherine smiled confidently. 'I have no intention of *promising* Sadler anything. If he should somehow get that impression . . .' she let her voice roll off as she shrugged innocently, '. . . well, I can't be held responsible for the way his feverish little mind works.' She glanced worriedly at the time again.

'He's going to be here any minute now. You're going to have to leave!'

'Nope.' Smitty shook his head emphatically. 'The more I hear about this plan of yours the less I like it. We're not leaving you alone to try it.'

'Oh yes, you are!' Catherine grabbed each of them by the arm and started them towards the front door. The doorbell rang. 'Oh lord,' she froze, 'he's here!' Doing a quick about-face, she began pulling them down the hallway towards the back door.

'I'll be right there, Sadler—just a minute!' She sang out sweetly over her shoulder, all the time tugging Smitty and Maggie closer to the back door. 'Don't worry,' she whispered hoarsely, 'I'm not crazy. I know what I'm doing, and I'm not going to get involved with Sadler—not any more than is absolutely necessary, and certainly *not* to the point where I have to jump into bed with him! But we were married, and that gives me a certain advantage that I'd be foolish not to take. Don't worry,' she repeated, 'I can handle Sadler.'

The doorbell rang again. 'I'm coming, I'm coming!' she shouted. 'Hang on just a second more, I'll be right there.' She opened the back door and pushed Maggie and Smitty out. 'And don't come back too soon!' She issued her order in tightly whispered tones and then with a quick wave closed the door on two very confused-looking people.

Running down the hallway, she hurried to the front door. Face flushed, eyes sparkling, hair slightly but enticingly disarrayed, she ran her tongue over her dry lips to moisten them, ran her sweaty palms down her hips to dry them, put on what she hoped was a sweet but alluring smile and opened the door. Only her ribcage stood witness to how wildly her heart pounded. She had a lot riding on the next hour or so. 'Hello, Sadler,' her breathlessness was very real, 'I'm sorry if I kept you waiting.'

Sadler's keen grey eyes at first widened when he saw

her, then narrowed tightly. 'The standard reason for taking that much time in answering the door is because you have to put something *on.*' His gaze raked her clinging robe. 'At least you're original.'

'But I didn't give you a reason yet!' Catherine was instantly on the defensive. 'I haven't said anything at all.'

'You didn't have to,' he cocked an amused eyebrow. 'I took it for granted. Or,' he paused, 'do you always answer the door undressed like that?'

'No, certainly not!' So far this wasn't going exactly the way she had it planned, and now thanks to his remark she felt completely selfconscious and clutched the bodice of her robe, narrowing the décolletage somewhat. 'If you'll let me explain,' she drew a shaky breath, 'I thought I'd have time to take a quick shower before you got here, but you must be early and . . .' she was trying desperately to salvage her plan, or what was left of it. '. . . and you caught me just as I was about to step into it. That's why I'm dressed like this,' she laughed nervously. 'I had to put something on to answer the door and that's why I took so long getting here.' She closed her eyes and muffled a dismayed groan—now she was doing too much explaining, and if she didn't shut up she would probably babble the whole thing to him. She drew a deep breath, forced a smile and looked up.

'Uh-huh.' He glanced past her into the apartment. 'Are you going to ask me in or are you going to keep me standing out here in the hallway with you looking like that?' He looked properly shocked. 'What *will* the neighbours think?'

'Of course, Sadler—come in.' It was a struggle, but Catherine managed to keep a smile on her face as she stepped aside to let him enter. As he walked past her she caught the scent of freshly applied aftershave lotion. It hadn't been so long that Catherine couldn't remember the scent of his aftershave, and the one he was wearing now wasn't the same one he had been using when they were married. A little frown slipped unnoticed across her face. How much else about Sadler had changed?

'Where is everybody?' Sadler's glance scanned the living-room, then came to a halt on Catherine as she closed the front door and started towards him. 'I thought Maggie was here,' he continued, his voice holding on to a note of uncertainty. 'When Smitty answered the phone he said he'd send Maggie to tell you. I thought if she was here she could take some notes for us—with your permission, of course,' she added dryly.

'She could,' Catherine agreed with a pleasant smile, 'if she were here—but she's not . . . here, I mean,' she shrugged apologetically.

'Oh?'

'Yes', she nodded, 'she and Smitty had a date this evening—dinner and a show, I think. In fact they were in such a rush to leave they couldn't stay to say hello.'

'Really?' For some reason Sadler seemed to find that amusing. 'Then we're alone in the apartment?'

Catherine swallowed hard, trying to relieve the tightness that had suddenly appeared in her throat. It wasn't so much *what* Sadler had said—that was innocent enough—it was the *way* he had said it, and the way he had looked when he said it. Instinctively she pulled the robe closer around her, wishing now she had gone with the three-piece pin-stripe suit instead.

'I expected you to be ripping mad by now,' confessed Sadler, his grey eyes following her every move, his lazy smile a visual indication of his appreciation of her robe and the way she had just tightened it.

If it is possible to blush from head to toe, Catherine did just that. 'I was mad,' she stammered, releasing the grip on her robe. 'I *am* mad, but I hope that the two of us are mature enough to deal with this situation in a civilised manner.'

'When were we ever civilised about anything, Cat?' he drawled, his gaze purposely lingering on the spots guaranteed to deepen Catherine's blush—and it did.

'White is definitely your colour,' he told her softly. 'You look good in it—damn good. Young, fresh, innocent—almost virginal.'

'It's an illusion, Sadler,' she replied with a tired smile. 'I don't feel young, fresh or innocent. And as for virginal,' she paused and her heart skipped a beat, 'you took care of that a long time ago.'

It was impossible to say the words without recalling the act, and for a moment their eyes locked and held, their thoughts like one as the atmosphere was charged with a sudden electricity. Her skin tingling, her pulse racing, it was Catherine who was the first to look away. 'What can I fix you to drink, Sadler?' She started towards the cabinet in the corner. 'Martini, wasn't it—very dry with a twist?'

'Scotch on the rocks,' he replied, smiling when she looked back surprised. 'Your memory's excellent, but tastes change, Cat,' he shrugged lazily. 'What I liked four years ago I don't necessarily enjoy now.'

As she turned away, her expression was tinged with concern. Was that remark supposed to have some definite point—besides the one about his taste in drinks? Knowing Sadler, she frowned. It probably did, but was it the obvious one—meaning her? There was only one way to find out.

'You're right, Sadler, lots of things change in four years.' She turned slowly and handed him his drink, giving him a good view of one long shapely leg half exposed through the slit in the robe. This time the look that crossed Sadler's face was one she recognised, and smiling to herself she turned, mentally chalking up one point for her side as she did. Not everything about Sadler had changed.

'So,' she drawled, sitting down slowly in a chair and crossing her legs, the fluffy pink ball on the open toe of her slippers being the target of her full attention, 'you've bought up the note.'

'That's right,' he nodded, his grey eyes keenly aware

for the first sign of anger from her, but Catherine had things well in hand—or so she thought. 'Like I told you on the phone,' he continued, 'the only thing that's changed as far you're concerned is that now you owe me the sixty-three thousand dollars and not the bank.'

'Now that you do have the note,' she pursed her lips, 'I don't suppose you'd consider extending the time? With a little more time it's possible I might be able to find a way to come up with the money, or some of it anyway. Maybe we could re-finance and . . .'

'No,' he shook his head, 'that's not possible. No extensions, Cat, I told you that.'

It was the answer she had expected, but even so it rankled. 'And if I can't pay it off?' She lowered her pale lashes to hide the expression she knew must be there in her eyes. Fury—loathing—resentment. 'What happens then?'

Sadler sat back against the sofa, taking time to consider Catherine's calm response. She was furious under that calm exterior, he knew her well enough to tell that, but she was also up to something—but what? 'The same thing that would have happened if the bank had held on to the note and you defaulted. I'll have to take the company in lieu of the money. Probably shut it right down and lay off the employees, sell off the assets if there are any.' He was deliberately baiting her, waiting to see what she'd do, but so far it wasn't working. With a look akin to admiration, he stared unnoticed at Catherine's profile before he continued. 'But there's no point in getting into all that now, you know as well as I do what could happen. But it doesn't have to happen that way, Cat. It's up to you.'

'What if I could come up with collateral?' She couched her words carefully; she had to be very, very cautious about how she handled this part of her plan.

'You must be referring to personal collateral of some kind, because the company's mortgaged to the hilt.'

Sadler looked surprised by her offer, but interested. 'That would amount to a considerable amount of collateral. What have you got that's worth that much?'

This was it—and with her stomach in knots so tight it hurt, her nerves so taut they felt as if they were burning through her skin, Catherine took her time in replying as she slowly re-crossed her legs, pretending she didn't see the slit in her white robe fall apart almost to her hipbone. Dipping her lashes once, she looked Sadler straight in the eye. 'I'm sure,' she purred silkily, her mouth forming a perfect pink pout, 'that if we put our heads together we could work out some sort of arrangement.'

For what seemed to her an eternity, Sadler's grey eyes kept their unflinching hold on her, then he did the one thing she hadn't considered: he laughed. 'Oh, Cat,' he chuckled, 'you never fail to amaze me! Just when I think I've got you all figured out you come up with something like this. It's Mata Hari, isn't it? Selling your favours for fun and profit.' He tossed his dark head back and laughed. 'I must be getting slow in my old age. I should have figured out that's what you were up to when you answered the door in that get-up. Oh, Cat,' he drawled, shaking his head slowly, 'do you really think you're worth sixty-three thousand dollars? I've already had you—and for nothing. Remember?'

Catherine did remember, and her resolve to remain calm vanished as she sprang from her chair like a hissing cat, her fists pummeling Sadler's chest as soon as she landed on him. 'Why, you . . . !'

'Ah, ah, ah,' he grabbed her wrists and stood up, shaking her warningly as he did. 'Nice girls don't use that kind of language!'

'Don't you patronise me, you . . . you . . .' she couldn't think of anything rotten enough as she struggled to get out of his grip.

'Now *this* is more what I expected,' he smiled down at her. 'Only I half expected to be attacked at the door.' He forced her arms straight down at her sides, holding her perfectly rigid in front of him. 'When you've got all this out of your system and you're ready to calm down,' he told her in a soft voice which only made her more furious, 'we'll talk about this matter—seriously.'

'We have nothing to say to one another!' she hissed breathlessly through clenched teeth, her breasts heaving with pent-up fury beneath the clinging white robe.

'We have plenty to say,' he countered, his grip still secure on her wrists. 'But if you don't want to do the talking, that's fine, but you're going to listen to what I have to say. Is that understood?' He gave her a little shake.

'Let go of me,' she warned tightly, her green eyes flashing.

He did just the opposite and tightened his grip. 'Are you going to listen to me?'

'How can I *not* listen to you, Sadler,' she returned hotly, 'when you're shouting in my ear! Now let go!'

'All right.' He dropped his hands and stepped back quickly out of her range. 'But let's drop all these silly little cat-and-mouse games and come right to the point. Whether you like it or not, I own your note. The bank, by the way,' he added with what could only be described as a smirk, 'was happy to get rid of it. Mr Cayhill was afraid they were going to have to eat Parker Plastics.'

Catherine opened her mouth to protest, but his slashing hand and angry black look stilled her. 'We both know you're not going to come up with that much money, not in three days, not in three years. I can wait until you default and foreclose,' he admitted, 'but I don't want to do it that way.'

'No?' she asked sarcastically.

'No! It's unnecessarily long and involved.' His lips thinned slightly. 'What I want is simply what I outlined in your office today. Look on me as an investor who wants . . .'

'Everything!' Catherine finished with an angry shake of her head. 'I've already heard your little offer, Sadler, and there's nothing simple about it. You want everything I have, everything my father . . .'

'Ran into the ground.' This time Sadler interrupted sharply. 'You sound like I'm taking over a profitable, flourishing company. It isn't. Parker Plastics is kaput—I don't know if even I can save it.'

'*Even* you!' Catherine tossed her head back and laughed. 'Don't tell me you have self-doubts about anything, Sadler? I thought you could do it all.' She threw herself back down in the chair. 'Why, Sadler,' she purred, her eyes slanted lazily like a cat's, 'this is a real red-letter day in my life. I'll have to mark it on my calendar so I never forget.'

'Are you all done ranting?' he asked patiently, one dark eyebrow arching quizzically. 'Because if you are I've got a dinner engagement, and I'd like to get this settled once and for all.'

'Ah, that's right,' Catherine's voice and eyes snapped. 'Sophia. You certainly wouldn't want to be late for that one!'

'No, I wouldn't,' he agreed easily, his mouth quirking with suppressed humour. 'So then . . . we're agreed that the simplest and least painful way to handle the takeover is the way I suggested. I'll get in touch with my attorneys tonight and we can probably get this all squared away in the morning—early afternoon at the latest.'

'No.'

Sadler's jaw snapped shut with an audible click, his eyes narrowing until they were only penetrating pinpoint balls of light. 'What did you say?'

'I said "no", Sadler.' Catherine calmly got to her feet. '*We* agreed to no such thing. I've got a few days to raise the money, and I'm at least going to try.'

'How, Cat?' Sadler's voice rang with angry frustration. 'You're only stalling for time. You've been trying to raise that much money for months and you haven't succeeded. What makes you think you can do in a few days what you haven't been able to do up to now?'

Catherine didn't have a ready answer. The plain fact was she didn't know what she was going to do. But one thing was certain, she wasn't going to hand everything over to Sadler without so much as a puppy whimper. 'I don't know, Sadler,' she admitted with a shrug, and as she did her robe slipped delicately off one shoulder, giving her a sudden idea. Leaving it there, she smiled at him. 'Maybe there's a way I haven't thought of—until now. I'll have to give it some serious thought.' She nodded soberly. 'I just might be able to raise the money after all.'

Her meaning was clear, and Sadler's expression hardened to one of barely controlled fury. 'Don't try it, *Catherine*,' he rarely called her Catherine. 'I'm warning you!'

'*You're* warning *me*!' Catherine's back went up. 'Who are you to be warning me about anything? You're the one who started all this, and in spite of your greatly inflated opinion of yourself,' she smiled tightly, 'you're not the only man around with money.'

'I'm the only man with money as far as you're concerned,' his voice was deadly serious.

'It's been four years, Sadler,' she replied, slowly drawling her words. 'Four *long* years. You stopped being the only man for me the day we were divorced.'

'Oh?' Sadler was now so angry a muscle danced uncontrollably alongside his jaw.

'Yes—*oh!*' she taunted. She knew he was furious, dangerously close to breaking point, but she couldn't stop herself. 'At one time you were the only man, Sadler,' she admitted, 'and you were an excellent teacher. I learned a great deal from you,' she smiled seductively. 'Life, love, and all those little things that make it interesting.'

Sadler's eyes narrowed until they were merely dark slits in a furious expression, the tiny anger lines around the corners of his eyes and at the sides of his mouth appearing like taut white scars. Catherine knew the look well—even though she had seen it only one time before. It was the same look he had had on his face the day she told him she was divorcing him, and it was a look she would never forget. Instinctively she began to withdraw, but it was already too late.

'All right, Cat,' he replied softly, the gentle tone of his voice in sharp contrast to the hard look in his eyes. 'If that's what you want, we'll do it your way. You've got yourself a deal. The money—all sixty-three thousand of it, free and clear, no strings attached—in exchange for *you*. You always were a quick study, so let's see what you've learned on your own in the past four years.' Like a coiled cobra, his arm shot out, his hand imprisoning her wrist in an iron grip. 'And for sixty-three thousand dollars, kitten,' he purred ominously, 'it had better be a *lot*. I think your bedroom's this way, isn't it?'

Temporarily stunned, Catherine stumbled blindly along behind him, her senses rapidly returning with every step he forced her to take. 'Don't be ridiculous, Sadler,' she found her voice and tugged at her arm. 'I'm not going anywhere with you.'

'Oh, yes, you are.' He didn't even bother to turn around as he spoke to her, merely pulled her along behind him. 'You just made me an offer too good to refuse, Cat, and I'm taking you up on it. Better me than someone else.'

Catherine had gone much too far with her charade and she knew it. 'But I wasn't serious, Sadler,' she stepped on his heel and stumbled into his hard-muscled back. 'You made me mad—I didn't mean it. I only said those things because . . .'

'That's too bad, Cat,' he finally glanced back over his shoulder, his jawline tensing when he saw the anxious look on her face, 'because I'm damn serious.'

They were in front of her bedroom door, and without so much as an uninterested glance at the doorknob, Sadler opened the door with a well-placed boot heel, kicking it open to the sounds of splintering wood.

'My door!' gasped Catherine, her eyes widening as he hauled her past it and into her bedroom. 'You've kicked a hole in my door!'

'Take it out of the sixty-three thousand dollars you're about to earn.' Sadler pulled her around in front of him, her door all but forgotten as she felt the edge of the bed touch the backs of her legs. Numb with disbelief, Catherine froze as he released her wrists and reached for the delicate white ribbon holding the bodice of her robe together.

'No, Sadler, don't!' she pleaded in earnest now, her hands ineffectually closing around his wide wrists, her fingers not even closing her grip. 'I didn't mean any of those things, you know I didn't.' He ignored her, his hands slipping through the now open robe to her breasts. 'Sadler . . . please . . .' She was no match for him physically and hot tears swelled against her eyelids, spilling slowly over her lashes and down her cheeks. 'Don't do this, Sadler,' she begged. 'I'll never forgive you. I'll hate you as long as I live, if you do!'

'But you already hate me, Cat,' his breath was a hot caress across her cheek, 'so I have nothing to lose.' His hands slid from her breasts to her waist and on to her hips, moulding her body against his.

For Catherine, the past four years vanished with a simple, fragile heartbeat, and it was yesterday again and she knew that this was what she had wanted from the moment she had seen Sadler at the restaurant. It was no wonder she had always given the impression of being 'cold' to any of the men she had dated since Sadler. How could she hope to have any sort of normal man/woman relationship with anyone of them when he had put a lock on her emotions and only he had the key?

With a gentle but forceful push, he toppled her over on to her bed, his own weight giving the bed an additional sway as he followed her down, pinning her unnecessarily beneath him. Unnecessarily, because Catherine wasn't going anywhere, she was exactly where she wanted to be, and *her* hands—hands that had just moments ago tried to push him away—now sought to draw him nearer.

Sadler's kiss when it came was almost brutal in its execution, his lips crushing down on hers, forcing her soft, willing lips apart. Catherine offered no resistance, indeed she had none, and instead supplied some encouragement of her own as her body moved sensually beneath his touch. 'Sadler . . .' She spoke his name softly—part whisper, part sigh. How many nights had she lain awake thinking of this very thing? The touch of his hands on her body, the taste of his lips on hers, the feeling of wanting someone so badly that it hurt. This was desire—this was Sadler.

At the sound of her voice Sadler raised his head slowly, the look of warm desire in his eyes darkening quickly to the colour of cold steel. 'What are you trying to pull now, Cat?' His voice was as cool as the look on his face. 'A moment ago you were begging me to stop, and now . . . this?' He rolled away from her and got to his feet, his expression filled with contempt as he stared down at her. 'When are you going to stop playing these stupid little games and be honest with *yourself* for a change, if with no one else? If you wanted me to make love to you why didn't you just say so, instead of putting both of us through all this foolishness?'

Catherine sat up with a snap, pulling her robe securely around her as she did. 'Don't make me laugh, Sadler!' She made quite a production of fastening her robe. 'You can't believe for one second that I actually *wanted* to make love to you? Ha!'

'Of course you did,' he growled, the tremor in his voice indicating his struggle for control, 'but that's the problem, and you won't admit it. You haven't faced an emotion honestly for one day in your life. Do you think you're somehow above the rest of us mortals and won't admit to a little lust? It hasn't been that long, Cat,' he shook his head slowly, the look on his face putting a sharp catch in her throat, 'that I can't remember the signs, so why this elaborate scheme of yours? Your considerable charms against my money? What was that supposed to prove,' he shrugged, 'that I still want you? All right,' his voice was still a little husky from their aborted lovemaking, 'I'll admit it—I do still want you. Now what?'

'Now you can get out!' Furious, Catherine was on her feet and shouting at him. 'Get out of my house! Get out of my life!' She pointed towards the door. 'Just get out!'

'Tomorrow morning, Catherine,' he clipped in city business tones. 'My attorney's office. I'll call you and tell when and where. Be there,' he warned.

Catherine's fingers closed around the nearest throwable object, which happened to be a small but expensive vial of perfume. *'Get out!'* This time her command was accompanied by the airborne bottle of perfume, missing his head by scant inches and shattering into a dozen pieces as it smashed against the door.

'At least your aim's improving,' he said coolly, glancing down indifferently at the shattered glass at his feet. 'But it doesn't change anything, Cat. You'll still hear from me in the morning.' He turned his back to her and opened the door.

'Go to hell, Sadler!' Catherine's voice trembled with rage.

'But I've never left, Cat,' he answered hollowly, a strange look on his face. He glanced back only one more time before he turned the corner and disappeared, the sound of the slamming front door echoing in Catherine's mind long after he had left.

CHAPTER FIVE

'WHAT in the world stinks?'

Catherine had heard Smitty's key in the front door lock and had hurried to greet them, but she was a second too late, and his question and curiously wrinkled nose brought a wry shrug to her shoulders. 'It's perfume,' she made a face.

'Perfume?' Smitty sniffed the air, then leaned down and sniffed her. 'It's not on you,' he straightened up and shook his head, 'it's everywhere. The whole place reeks of it!' He started down the hallway, a curious Maggie and a frowning Catherine hot on his heels. 'The smell's coming from your room.'

'I know. I—er—I couldn't get it off the door.' With a sudden burst of speed Catherine passed them. There was a little more to be explained here than the scent of perfume and she hurried to get ahead of them, trying to block—or at least put off—their view of her bedroom door. She wasn't successful.

'What's that?' they demanded, their puzzled voices and pointing fingers as one.

This was clearly one of those questions that demanded a lengthy and detailed explanation, but Catherine delayed as long as she could by choosing the more obvious reply. 'It's a hole,' she stated.

'We can see that, Catherine,' frowned Smitty. 'What we want to know is how it got there and why.' He wrinkled his nose again. 'I suppose there's a connection between *it* and the perfume?'

'Sort of,' Catherine's admission was accompanied by an attempt at an innocent smile. 'It was an accident. Not the hole,' she added quickly, 'that was deliberate, but the perfume was an accident. It hit the door by mistake.'

She stopped right there and smiled again. Maybe they'd accept that? There was no point in going into a lot of detail, like how the hole had got there and why. Maggie and Smitty had both been opposed to her plan this evening right from the start, and if she had to explain about the hole, then she'd have to explain why Sadler was in her bedroom in the first place, and that was something she would just as soon not do. 'So how was your evening?' she asked.

'You're kidding!' Maggie's eyebrows arched as she pushed open the door and stepped inside Catherine's aromatic bedroom. 'The answer to that has to be dull by comparison. Let me get this straight,' she paused. 'If the perfume hit the door by mistake, I think it's safe to assume the original target was something else.' She held her breath. 'What?'

'Sadler,' Catherine smiled. 'His head, to be exact. My aim was a little off,' she shrugged.

'I think I'd better sit down for the rest of this, I'm not as young as I used to be,' Maggie groaned lightly as she sank down on the tiny chair just inside the bedroom door. 'I'm almost afraid to ask, but I will—what happened?'

'Nothing,' Catherine shrugged.

'Nothing?' Smitty echoed Catherine's reply in disbelief. 'As in "not a thing"?' He wagged an accusing finger at the door. 'With a hole in the bottom of your door big enough to drive a truck through and the whole apartment smelling like something out of the Arabian Nights, you actually expect us to believe that "nothing" happened here this evening? Catherine,' he shook his head slowly, '*really!*'

'I think I should tell you something, Catherine,' Maggie sighed as she glanced round the room. 'After you told us what you had in mind for Sadler tonight, I almost expected to come back here and find a body on the floor—yours, probably—but you're obviously all right. Does that mean . . .' she lowered her voice to a library whisper, 'Sadler's not . . .' fearful of what she might find, Maggie's brown eyes searched furtively across the floor.

'Dead?' Catherine finished Maggie's question for her, rolling the word deliciously around her tongue and savouring every last drop. 'Not yet,' her expression hardened. 'But don't think the idea hasn't occurred to me this evening, because it has. And there's not a court in the land that would convict me,' her voice rose dramatically to match her waving hand. 'It would be a clear case of justifiable homicide if there ever was one. I might even get a medal!'

'I think we're getting a little off the track.' Smitty turned and started down the hallway towards the kitchen, indicating with a gesture that the two women should follow him, which they did. 'We can only deal with one disaster at a time,' he continued, 'so let's forget the hole in your door—and the perfume—for the time being,' he sliced in dryly, and Catherine knew what that meant, 'and get right to what Sadler has in mind for Parker Plastics. What's he going to do about the company?' A sudden thought brought a pair of grey brows arching sharply together. 'I'm assuming, of course, that the two of you got around to talking about the company. That *was* why he came over, wasn't it?'

'Oh, we talked about it all right,' Catherine ran her hand tiredly across her eyes. 'Maybe I should say Sadler talked about it, I just listened. Sadler has decided that the simplest way is for me to sign everything over to him first thing in the morning. No muss, no fuss, no bother. It's so messy,' she drawled bitterly, 'if we have to go through the courts with a foreclosure.'

'Tomorrow morning?' Smitty looked surprised. 'What happened to the few days you had left?'

'Oh, I still have them,' nodded Catherine, her fingers tapping nervously on the kitchen table, 'at least theoretically. But Sadler's so damn sure of himself—*and* of me—that he's already decided I can't come up with the money. He's making plans for me to meet him in his lawyers' office tomorrow morning.' She allowed herself a small smile. 'Won't he be surprised!'

'You're not going to go?' asked Smitty.

'No.' This much Catherine was certain. 'I've got three days and I'm taking every last second of them, whether Sadler likes it or not—and I hope he doesn't. I've been sitting here thinking,' she paused thoughtfully, 'that if I can find a way to raise most of the money for Sadler maybe I could get the bank to give me a personal loan for the balances.'

Maggie began to laugh. 'You don't mean poor Mr Cayhill? After all he's gone through with you, you've actually got the nerve to ask him for more money?'

'Yes!' Catherine didn't see anything *that* funny. 'He got his money, didn't he?'

'Sure he did,' Maggie's eyes widened at Catherine's reasoning, 'but Sadler gave it to him—you didn't.'

'Well, this would be different,' Catherine pursed her lips. 'And I think I've figured out a way to swing it. I can sell my car, cash in my life insurance . . .' her green eyes suddenly gleamed. Here in front of her were two potential investors. 'How much life insurance do the two of you have?'

'Good lord!' Maggie closed her eyes and covered her heart with her hand. 'She's planning on killing us for the insurance money!'

'Don't be ridiculous,' laughed Catherine. 'I wondered how much of a cash-in value they had. Smitty offered me what he had saved and if we all pool our resources maybe we can . . .'

'*Catherine!*' Smitty's voice was as stern as Catherine had ever heard him. 'Just listen to yourself!' he scowled. 'You're going off the deep end about this. Even if Maggie and I did all that, and you sold your car, we still couldn't raise sixty-three thousand dollars,' he shook his head soberly. 'Or nowhere near that amount, and you know it.'

Catherine closed her eyes and sighed, letting her head droop forward on to her arms. 'I do know that, Smitty,' she whispered. 'It's just that I hate letting Sadler get his own way about this. He waltzes back into my life and just like *that*,' she snapped her fingers. 'He's taking over again. When he's through with me I won't have a thought or a feeling I can call my own. I hate it!' her voice trembled with emotion. 'I can't tell you how much I hate it—and *him*!'

'I know,' Smitty frowned lightly. 'You've told all of us that so many times I'm beginning to think you believe it yourself. But what can you do? Realistically, I mean. Are you going to meet him in the morning at his lawyers' like he expects?'

'No.' Catherine shook her head, the look on her face one of unshakeable determination. 'I've made up my mind about that. Maybe there's nothing I can do to prevent him from ultimately taking over the company, but I can make him wait the entire three days before he does it. And that's precisely what I intend to do,' she smiled. 'Sadler hates to wait for anything!'

'Well?' At the sound of the slamming back door Smitty glanced up. 'How'd it go?'

'Exactly the way Sadler wanted it.' Catherine, her eyes a deep, almost emerald green, stood with her back pressed to the door, her well-shaped mouth pale in a downward cast, her slim shoulders sagging in a dejected droop. 'As of ten o'clock this morning Sadler is now in complete charge of Parker Plastics. I wonder if he's going to change the name to McQuade Plastics?' She let her voice trail off unemotionally, then slowly shook her head. 'It doesn't have quite the same ring to it as *Parker* Plastics, does it? Oh well . . .' she sat down with a soft plop into one of the kitchen chairs, then resting her elbows on the table she propped her chin up in her hands and stared across the room at Smitty. 'At least I made him wait the whole three days,' her victorious smile was a pale carbon copy of what she hoped it would be, 'that's *something*, anyway.'

'If you say so,' shrugged Smitty, his back to her, his hands in the sink peeling vegetables. 'So what's going to happen now?'

'What happens now?' Catherine echoed his question slowly, punctuating it with several deep sighs. 'Now Sadler moves into my father's office. I should say *my* office,' her lip curled into an unpleasant sneer. 'He was generous enough to give me an entire week to move all my "non-essentials"—and that's a direct quote from the lips of Sadler McQuade—to move my non-essentials out of my father's office and into an office of my own.' Here her voice hardened noticeably. '*Office* is Sadler's word for the broom closet down the hall. Naturally Sadler wants the front office for himself *and* he wants Maggie as well.' She shrugged absently. 'I suppose I should be grateful that he didn't decide to give me the little room in the basement—the one in back of the boiler, with no window and a bare bulb on the ceiling.'

Smitty turned around, his eyes filling wide with surprise. 'You don't mean to tell me he's going to assume the actual running of the company, when he's involved with so many other things as well?' His expression creased with concern. 'I got the impression that this was strictly a money deal on his part. Oh, I know what he said,' he added quickly when he saw Catherine begin to reply, 'but I thought that after taking care of the financial end he'd bow out and leave the day-to-day running of the firm to you.'

'Me?' Catherine forced a bitter laugh. 'Actually,' she scowled, 'that very idea did come up in today's meeting—by his own lawyers, actually—but Sadler vetoed it right away. It seems he has his doubts as to my administrative ability. That's why he's decided to take charge. It's amazing when you think about it,' her voice trailed off slightly, 'that Sadler can find the time in his busy schedule to squeeze in the running of Parker's—what with his cattle and his electronics and his mini-conglomerate and whatever else he's got his sticky fingers into. Amazing . . .' she repeated the word slowly. 'That's Sadler all right—the *amazing* Sadler McQuade.'

Smitty dried his hands and sat down opposite her at the kitchen table, his face a picture of studied concern. 'After everything that's happened to you lately, Catherine,' he said in a soft voice, 'I've got to say that you're taking all this very calmly.'

'Yes, I am,' she agreed with a stiff nod. 'For the past few days I've been so furious with Sadler I could have chewed nails every time I thought of him. And yet, when I signed the papers this morning and he became in charge of everything, it was as if someone had snuffed out the flame and I was the candle. I'm all burned out, Smitty,' her forehead creased deeply. 'I'm cold, stiff and non-combustible. I haven't anything left to give. That's it,' she sighed. 'It's over. It doesn't matter to me any more.'

'Of course it matters,' Smitty reached for her hand and squeezed it reassuringly. 'No matter what Sadler does or doesn't do it's still your company. *Your* Parker's—not Sadler's.'

'No, not really,' she shook her head slowly. 'Oh, Sadler's worked out some sort of arrangement where I stand to profit if and when the company does, but that just looks good on paper. Parker's the name on the building, but that's all. It's Sadler's money, Sadler's business, Sadler's problems. In a way,' she sighed softly, 'I'm glad it's all over.'

Smitty got to his feet, hiding his deep feeling of concern behind a pleasant smile. 'Have you eaten anything yet?'

'No,' Catherine shook her head. 'Sadler suggested it, but I wasn't in the mood for a celebration lunch, especially with him—so I told him no.'

'Good,' nodded Smitty. 'Then you can eat with me

before you go back to the office. What do you feel like? A nice salad maybe,' he suggested, 'with a bowl of homemade soup? How's that sound?'

'No, nothing,' Catherine shook her head. 'I'm not hungry.'

'But you've got to eat *something*,' Smitty protested, Catherine's pale complexion a worry. 'You haven't eaten enough lately to keep a baby chick alive. If you don't want a salad and a bowl of soup then how about a sandwich—a bacon, lettuce and toma . . .' He stopped talking; Catherine was on her feet and leaving the kitchen. 'Where are you going?'

'To bed.'

'To bed?' Smitty was surprised. 'But what about your lunch? What about the office?'

'I'm not hungry, Smitty,' Catherine repeated. 'Maybe I'll have something to eat later. And as far as the office is concerned,' Maggie can take care of anything that comes up.' Her hand twitched nervously at her side. 'She knows as much about the business as I do, maybe more.'

'OK,' Smitty agreed; he didn't really have much choice. 'Maybe you're right. A few hours' rest today might do you a world of good. I'll just call Maggie and let her know that you won't be in the office this afternoon.'

'Fine.' Catherine's voice was as dead and listless as the tiny wave of her hand. 'You do that. And while you're at it, Smitty,' she sighed, 'maybe you'd better tell her I might not be in tomorrow either. In fact . . .' she paused, the tiny lines of worry and exhaustion on her face more prominent than they had ever been. 'The more I think about it, the more I like not going back to Parker's at all. There's nothing there for me any more, Smitty. It's not mine, it's Sadler's.'

'You can't do that, Catherine,' he shook his head.

'Sure I can,' she disagreed, her eyes narrowing slightly. 'Sadler wanted Parker Plastics—well, now he's got it. So let him run it—Maggie'll help him.'

'That's not what I meant,' frowned Smitty. 'I meant you can't do that because it's not fair. It's not fair to Maggie, it's not fair to Sadler, and most of all it's not fair to you. You've got more class than that, honey. If you've got to bow out, bow out with some style.'

'Style?' Smitty's criticism didn't hit the mark, and Catherine just shrugged. 'Sadler's got enough style for the two of us. In fact he probably got enough style for the entire world. I'm tired, Smitty,' she admitted. 'I'm tired of worrying about Parker's, I'm tired of worrying about Sadler, I'm just . . . plain . . . tired.'

Catherine turned and headed towards her bedroom. She was doing more than retreating from an unpleasant situation, she was retreating from the world.

Like an injured animal might seek the quiet sanctuary of its den, Catherine darkened her bedroom by pulling her curtains, undressed and crawled into bed, ostensibly to lick her wounds and mend herself. But her wounds were emotional, not physical, and as such were more difficult to heal.

Losing Parker's, of course, had been a terrible blow, but what had finally tipped the scales was losing it to Sadler. If only it had been anyone else . . . she shivered and pulled the covers up tighter around her . . . anyone at all.

Lying here now it seemed to her that the two most important events in her life—her marriage to Sadler and running Parker Plastics—had both failed miserably. She'd like to blame Sadler for both failures, but that would be too easy and only partially correct. He had picked up Parker's only *after* it had failed, but was it her fault that it had failed? Their marriage had been more complicated, and while Sadler certainly was the cause of the divorce, did she have to accept the blame that it had failed?

She shivered again, and not from the cold. In the four years since the divorce she had never admitted, not even to herself, that perhaps it wasn't all Sadler's fault. At the time, however, it had all seemed so cut and dried to her; Sadler had been unfaithful, Sadler was to blame.

Oddly enough, or perhaps not, Sophia Blair came to mind, and her reaction to seeing Sadler for the first time in the restaurant. Catherine understood it—and resented it—because it was almost identical to her own. Resented, she told herself, not jealousy. She had no reason to be jealous. He was a free agent, he could stir as many hearts as he wanted to, just as long as it wasn't hers. Not any more—that one time had been enough.

Catherine's pale lips formed into a reluctant smile. She couldn't help but recall the first time she had seen Sadler. She had smiled then, just like Sophia, and the memory was so strong now that it made her smile again.

Catherine had accompanied her father to one of those business luncheons where half the business conducted had nothing to do with the business at hand. Bored and looking for something to relieve the tedium, her mildly inquisitive gaze checked out the people around her. It only took her a second to find Sadler. Surrounded by women, their eyes glued on his every word, Sadler nevertheless felt another pair of eyes on him and glanced up, returning Catherine's luminous green gaze with an interest of his own.

She smiled, he smiled, then he excused himself from the small gathering around him and began to make his way over to her. In that split instant in time, shorter than it takes to blink an eye, Catherine had finally seen the man of her dreams and decided she wanted him. And at nineteen she had yet to be told she couldn't have everything she wanted. She wanted Sadler, ergo Sadler was hers. It was as simple as that.

Was it really that simple, or had she been incredibly naïve? Unrealistic perhaps, or just so much in love with the perfect man that when his imperfections began to show they were immediately blown up out of all proportions.

But at the time it *was* perfect—and wonderful as well.

A week is not very long to get to know someone, but by the end of the first week Catherine knew all she needed to know about Sadler McQuade. She loved him and she wanted to marry him, so much so she had done the proposing. Actually, she had been so sure of herself that it wasn't even a suggestion that they marry—it had been a demand. A demand that at first took Sadler by surprise. Then he had laughed, that low soft laugh he had that always reminded Catherine of the purring of a large contented cat—part amusement, part satisfaction. 'So you think we should get married?' His grey eyes sparkled with an expression to this she didn't understand. 'All right, Cat,' he nodded. 'If that's what you want, that's what you'll get.' And a scant week later they were married.

Perhaps it was because the courtship had been so easy that the marriage seemed so difficult by comparison. But whatever the reason for the disillusionment, eight months later a bitter Catherine was filing for divorce. Sadler had turned every young girl's dreams of love and marriage and forever-after into a nightmare. Destroying a marriage was one thing—destroying a dream was totally different, and for that reason alone Catherine could never forgive him. Every hope, every plan she ever made had been destroyed by the man she loved. But who else *but* the man you loved could do that? No one else in the world had that power.

And it had been so perfect a beginning. No woman could have asked for a gentler lover. Men as lovers are not naturally gentle, they have a tendency to be heavy-handed. They have to be taught the gentle hand, and they have to be taught that by a woman. That Sadler already knew a soft touch came as no surprise to Catherine. If she wanted to be honest with herself she would have to admit that his obvious experience with women was a part of his fascination. But once Sadler had said 'I do' it meant 'I don't'—at least not with other women, and that was when the trouble began.

It wasn't all other women, Catherine admitted to herself now in retrospect. It was Sadler himself. When they were married he was at a time in his career when he had to work harder, not less. On an intellectual level Catherine understood that, but for a brand-new bride, still thrilled with her husband and her life, it soon became a bitter pill to swallow.

What was more important to him, his business or his wife? Not a fair question, but a question Catherine found herself asking more and more during their brief marriage. And Sadler had tried to make it up to her, but in the end even those few times were ruined.

Like their camping trip to Canada . . . memories flooded in now, and Catherine let them. Left to their own devices on a small lake in Canada, they had had a tent, two sleeping bags and one another. And for two days it was all she could have asked for—holding hands and watching the moonlight dance across the still water, listening to the strange forest sounds, and trying and finally succeeding in making love in a single sleeping bag. Not even the rain dampened her spirits—what had killed it was the sight and the sound of the seaplane coming at them out of the sun. She knew immediately what it meant and so did Sadler; some business emergency was about to turn a week into two days. It wasn't fair, and Catherine resented it.

So once again Sadler was in the position of trying to make it up to her, this time by taking her to South America for what was supposed to be a month of long warm lazy days on his ranch. But somehow he had neglected to tell her about his neighbour—or more to the point, his neighbour's daughter, the beautiful dark-eyed Teresa Maria, who was as obviously surprised to meet Catherine as Catherine was to meet her. '*Esposa?*' the beauty had pouted, but ever so delicately. 'I did not know you had taken a wife, Sadler.' She pronounced the *a* as *ah* and the *e* as *a*, making it all sound beautifully breathless. 'It was sudden—no?' Dark eyes peered from under long black lashes as she looked for the first signs of a thickening waist on Catherine.

Catherine just smiled back, because Sadler hadn't made love to her until they were married, and it wasn't because she hadn't been willing. As it turned out it was about the only thing Catherine had in Argentina to smile about.

Churlishly and perhaps childishly, Catherine had spent practically every minute in their bedroom. Teresa could ride; Catherine couldn't. Teresa knew everyone there was to know; Catherine didn't and refused to make an effort. What Catherine was trying to do was drive Sadler away from Teresa and towards her—what she accomplished was exactly the opposite. If she could go back and do something differently, she sighed regretfully, she'd certainly do that differently.

'Catherine?' Smitty pushed open the door and stepped inside her bedroom, the still pitch-black room and eerie silence putting an unseen frown on his face. 'Are you asleep?'

'No,' Catherine shook her head weakly. 'I feel so tired—that's why I came to bed, but I can't sleep.'

'Do you know you've been in here since yesterday afternoon?' It was a question that required no answer, and Catherine gave none. 'Don't you think it's about time you got up? You might feel better if you do.'

'I thought about it,' she admitted in a toneless voice. 'But then I realised I have nothing to get up for, so why should I bother?'

'That's ridiculous!' Smitty's worry caused him to snap at her. 'Not only is that untrue, it's also self-pitying, and that's not like you. In fact,' he gestured, 'none of this nonsense is you. A day or two at home to sit around and relax is one thing, but you haven't been out of that bed since you came back from the lawyer's office!'

'Lawyer's office?' she thinned her lips. 'Don't remind me! That's one day in my life I'm trying to forget.'

'Why?' Smitty stared at her. 'You gave it your best

shot, Catherine. You couldn't do any more than that. You've nothing to regret.'

'Don't I?' She smiled thinly at him, his slender form standing in stark relief in the doorway of her bedroom. She had so many regrets she didn't know where to begin. Maybe if she had done things differently with Sadler, maybe if she had done things differently with Parker's, maybe, maybe, maybe . . .

'Catherine?'

'What, Smitty?' she sighed.

'I was going over to Maggie's this evening, but perhaps I should . . .'

'No, no,' Catherine shook her head, 'you don't need to stay here and hold my hand. I'm fine. If I need anything I know where it is.'

'There's sliced cold roast beef in the refrigerator,' he made it sound yummy, obviously trying to tempt her into eating something. 'I could fix you a plate before I go?'

'No, thank you,' she smiled faintly. 'If I'm hungry I'll go get it. Give Maggie my love.'

For a moment Smitty hesitated, then reluctantly agreed. 'All right, Catherine. Good night.'

'Sadler's on the phone . . . *again*.' Smitty stood in the open doorway to Catherine's bedroom, one hand on his hip, the other hand on the doorknob. 'What do you want me to tell him this time?'

'I don't care what you tell him, Smitty,' her reply sounded muffled. 'Tell him I'm asleep and that I don't want to be disturbed . . . ever.'

'I've already told him that,' he replied slowly, the worried note in his voice becoming more obvious. 'I've been telling him *that* plus assorted other excuses for three days now. He's beginning to think I'm either plain crazy or a pathological liar—and I can't say that I blame him.'

'What do I care what Sadler McQuade thinks about anything? But if you're so worried,' sighed Catherine, 'then don't answer the phone. That way you won't have to tell him anything. That's what I'm doing,' she smiled thinly, 'and it's working.' Her smile was as pale and wan as it could be and disappeared almost as quickly as it had appeared, her expression returning to the strange blank stare she had developed lately. It was an expression that Smitty decided couldn't go on any longer.

'I'm calling the doctor.' Smitty's face hardened with resolve. 'Enough is enough, Catherine. A little rest is one thing, but if you're sick enough to stay in bed for three days, then you're sick enough to be in hospital.'

'Sick?' She was insulted. 'I'm not sick!'

'No? Well, what do you call it?' he gestured. 'Your room's as dark as the bottom of a coalmine. You've eaten practically nothing and you haven't been out of bed in days. If that's not sick, what is it?'

'I'm not sick, Smitty,' she repeated, her voice a hoarse whisper. 'I'm tired, that's all. Just tired.'

'No, Catherine,' his sober expression never changed as he shook his head in flat denial, 'there's more to it then simply being tired. The first day, maybe,' he conceded, 'but not now, not after all this time. I hate doing this, Catherine,' his voice faltered briefly but came back stronger than ever, 'but if you're not up and dressed and in the kitchen ready to eat something in fifteen minutes, I'm calling the doctor.'

'You can't order me around like that!' Catherine fought back, her voice snapping with some of its usual life. 'This is my home and I'll do what I want to—including staying in bed. I'm warning you, Smitty,' she waggled a finger at him, 'if you call the doctor, after I specifically told you not to, you're . . . you're *fired*!'

The expression that crossed Smitty's face aged him ten years. 'You won't fire me, Catherine,' he said softly, 'and we both know it.'

Tears welled up in her eyes. 'No, I won't, Smitty. How can I—you're the only one who puts up with me, but don't call the doctor, *please*.' Her voice was so soft he could hardly hear her. 'I'll eat something, I promise I will, but don't make me get up. Not yet, I'm still so tired.'

It was a small concession on her part, but if she carried out her promise to eat something at least it was a step in the right direction. 'All right,' Smitty frowned his agreement, 'as long as you eat a good dinner tonight I won't call the doctor, at least not now. But if you're not up for good in the morning, Catherine . . .' he purposely left the rest of his threat unspoken, but she knew what he meant.

When she first heard the sound of Sadler's voice she just assumed it was part of her current dream—dreams, daydreams or memories, they were all the same—and Sadler was a part of every one of them. But when his voice became louder and stronger she realised he was in the hallway just outside her bedroom door talking to Smitty. She frowned and turned over, burying her face in the mattress under the pillow a little like an ostrich might bury its head in the sand.

Without so much as a courtesy knock the door to her bedroom flew open, banging against the wall with enough force to jar the bed. 'Don't stand on ceremony, Sadler,' she snapped, 'just barge right in! And I hope you know somebody in the wholesale door business,' she continued to mutter out of the corner of her mouth, 'Because if that door's broken and I have to replace it *again* . . .'

'To hell with the door,' he roared from the doorway. 'What are you doing in bed? And why is it so damn dark in here?' He started towards the heavily covered windows.

'I'm in bed because I'm sleeping,' she clipped icily. 'Or I was until you barged in.' From the corner of her eye she saw his head turn towards the window and knew what he had in mind. 'Don't touch those drapes!' But it was too late—he had already thrown them open, the last of the day's twilight filtering softly into her bedroom.

'Close those drapes!' she ordered, covering her head with her pillow.

He ignored her demand, dismissing it with a single cocked eyebrow. 'I've called you at least a dozen times in the past few days.' His boot heels snapped angrily against the floor as he marched towards her. 'Why didn't you have the common decency to return even one?'

'I've been busy,' she muttered.

'Doing *what*?' he exclaimed.

'That's none of your business,' she iced. 'Your business is Parker Plastics and the running thereof. So go do it, and get out of my bedroom!'

'Ah! That's what this is all about, isn't it, Cat?' Hands on his lean hips, a disgusted scowl on his face, Sadler stood by the side of her bed and slowly shook his head. 'You couldn't cut the mustard in your role of business tycoon, so you don't want anybody else to succeed. A change in script is in order, eh, Cat?' He glanced at her sheet-covered form. 'What is it this time, the death scene from *Camille*? You're very good, but where's your cough?'

'If I thought you were worth the effort, Sadler,' Catherine mumbled into her pillow, 'I'd get up and slap your face for that.'

For the next few moments he just stared at her, her face still pressed against the mattress where he couldn't see it, her shoulder-length red hair a bright explosion of colour against the white pillowcase. Slowly Sadler's expression changed from displeasure to uncertainty to concern. 'Turn over, Catherine,' he ordered firmly. 'I'm tired to listening to you talk to me through the mattress.'

'Then you're missing the whole point here, Sadler,' she picked up her chin just enough to unscramble her words. 'I don't want to talk to you at all. Go away.'

'I said to turn over,' he repeated his demand, and reached for the sheet covering her, pulling it back to her waist. When she still didn't move he grabbed hold of her shoulders, momentarily surprised to feel the pronounced delicate bones beneath his hands. Using only what slight strength was necessary to turn her over, he gently rolled her on to her back, his hands slipping almost instantly away. Once on her back, Catherine folded her arms across her chest, squinted her green eyes and glared at him.

'My God,' gasped Sadler, his eyes wide as saucers, 'you look like hell!'

'Thank you!' she snapped. 'It must be this new shade of lipstick. Do you really like it?'

'I'm not kidding, Cat,' he lowered his voice, 'I only wish I were. When's the last time you looked at yourself in a mirror?—not lately, I'll bet.' He glanced quickly around the room, spotted a hand mirror on the night-stand next to her bed, reached for it and held it up in front of her. 'Well?'

Catherine was surprised by what she saw. She was more than surprised, she was startled, because the face in the mirror didn't look anything like her. 'Well, I . . .' she stammered weakly, 'I've been . . .' She stopped suddenly, for she'd been about to say she'd been 'sick', but how could she claim that now after the argument she'd just had with Smitty about that very thing? She frowned and changed it to, 'I've been sleeping, and so what if my hair needs combing—what am I supposed to look like? I don't usually wake up to comb my hair just so I can go back to sleep.'

Sadler reached for the hairbrush that was also on the night-stand and sitting down on the edge of her bed he began to slowly draw it through a tangled lock of long red hair. 'When Smitty called me,' he talked while he gently brushed, 'I thought he was exaggerating. I remember your flair for the dramatic and I thought this was just your latest attempt to drive me crazy. I can see now that I was wrong, and for that I apologise.'

Catherine quietly endured his strong hands trying to brush gently through her hair. Her reflection in the mirror had been a shock, to say the least, and since her hair needed brushing and she didn't have the energy or inclination to do it, it might as well be Sadler. 'There's nothing wrong with me.' She tried to shake her head, but a firm tug on her hair stopped her in a hurry. 'Smitty had no business calling you, and I'm going to tell him so!'

'You're not going to tell Smitty anything of the sort,' Sadler's voice was softly hypnotic. 'He was worried about you.' With the lightest of touches he removed a stubborn strand of hair that was clinging to her cheek, holding it between his fingers as he did. 'You always did have the silkiest hair,' he murmured almost to himself, apparently fascinated by the lock in his hand. 'I used to love it when you wore it loose. Some of it always managed to be on my shoulder in the morning.'

Catherine automatically stiffened, her expression tightening warily. 'Now that you *are* here, Sadler,' she replied, 'what exactly is it that you want?'

The spell was broken and he reluctantly released the strand of hair, his attention all serious as he noted her pale complexion, her dull, almost lifeless green eyes and what appeared to be smudgy coloured circles beneath them. Catherine's flair for the dramatic aside, this was no act. Sadler smiled and stood up. 'Right now I want to have a little talk with Smitty about something.' He tossed her the hairbrush. 'Finish brushing your hair. I'll be right back.'

'Sure,' she curled her lip, 'and I know what you want to talk to Smitty about, you want to talk about *me*. The two of you will put your pointed little heads together and decide there's something wrong with me. Well, I'm telling you there isn't!'

'What makes you think I want to talk about you?' He cocked an arrogant eyebrow. 'And you called *me* an egotist? You're not that fascinating a subject, my dear,' he shook his head. 'It just so happens I'd like a cup of coffee.'

'Liar!'

'Don't go away,' he grinned. I'll be right back.'

She made a face at his back as he started to leave, but he quickly glanced back, saw her and laughed. His laugh, however, was shortlived, having vanished completely by the time he turned and shut the door to her bedroom.

Her hairbrush still in her lap, Catherine kept her gaze fixed at the last spot she had seen Sadler, his and Smitty's voices only garbled noises in the hallway beyond her bedroom. Sadler's voice sounded sharp to her as if raised in anger, but what did he have to be angry about? And Smitty's voice, always quiet—always reassuring. She couldn't understand the words, but she didn't have to. They were talking about her and she knew it.

Why had Smitty called Sadler, of all people? Didn't he know she was trying to forget him? It was bad enough his being the subject of her every dream and thought, without him being here in person. She didn't need him or want him, and she'd tell Sadler exactly that when he came back!

A rap sounded on her door and her expression came to life. He was back, and no matter what the two of them had hatched up, she wasn't going to do it. The gleam of battle fresh in her eyes, she stared at the door. 'Come in, Sadler.'

The door opened and Smitty stepped in.

'Oh, it's you.' Her face fell.

'Thank you.' Smitty's quick smile covered an anxious eye. 'I think I've heard better greetings than that!'

'You know what I mean,' she waved her hand, surprised to find the hairbrush still in it. 'I thought it was what's-his-name.'

'What's-his-name's left.' Smitty brought over a cup of tea and a plate of freshly baked cookies. 'I thought you might like something to eat for a change.'

'I've eaten!' Indignant, she glared at him.

'If that's what you want to call it,' he shrugged. 'I call it sitting at the table in a tattered bathrobe pushing food around your plate. The only food missing was what you spilt over the side.'

'Never mind all that,' she scowled. 'I got up, didn't I? I want to know what he said.'

'Who?'

'Sadler!' she snapped impatiently. 'I know the two of you were out there in the kitchen hatching up something. I want to know what it was.'

'It doesn't matter,' he shook his head, 'because I told him it wouldn't work anyway.'

'Good!' She pursed her lips with smug satisfaction. 'I'm glad you did.' She paused. 'What wouldn't work?'

'Sadler had two suggestions,' replied Smitty. 'One was the same as mine—call the doctor.'

'Ohh!' Catherine looked as if she was about to scream.

'Let me finish,' he held up his hand. 'I said he had two suggestions. He has a friend who has a cabin in the Monogahelas, below the Dolly Sods around the Spruce Knob area. It's isolated, quiet, no phone, no distractions.' He paused as if in anticipation of her reaction to what he was about to say next. 'He said if you were going to push yourself into a nervous breakdown that was the place to do it.'

'Nervous breakdown!' Catherine's eyes flared. 'What's he doing now, practising medicine on the side?' She drew her lips into a tightly controlled smile. 'He'd like that, wouldn't he—to see me a crumbled mess. Just one more scalp on his belt.' She paused and nibbled thoughtfully on her lower lip for a moment. 'Does he really think I'm having a nervous breakdown?'

'Well, Catherine,' he gestured sympathetically, 'what would you think if I described your actions to you but said it was somebody else? I don't think you're that bad yet,' he shrugged, 'but something has to be done, and I think that's what Sadler had in mind when he suggested the cabin. He's worried about you, Catherine,' his voice softened. 'We all are.'

For a moment her expression reflected deep concentration, so deep she reached without thinking for a cookie and dunked it in her hot tea. 'Do you think I should go?' she asked, plopping the now soggy cookie in her mouth.

'That's up to you, Catherine,' Smitty shook his head. 'But you've got to do something to snap out of this. Either go to the cabin or take a vacation or go back to the office and help . . .'

'No. If Sadler's running into problems at the office and needs help,' she smiled nastily, 'that's tough.'

'No, that's childish,' he reprimanded harshly.

Her cheeks burned from the truth of his statement, but she shook her head as if she didn't care. 'Call it anything you want to, Smitty, I'm not going in. Sadler steps in, buys up Parker's, crowns himself head, then expects me to . . .'

'To do what?' Smitty's brows arched curiously. 'Pull your own weight? If it were anyone but Sadler who bought Parker's you wouldn't be able to do enough for them, but since it is Sadler you're doing nothing to help. That sounds like a mighty big case of sour grapes to me. What are you really afraid of, Catherine?' he asked gently. 'Are you worried you're going to have to finally admit that you're still in love with Sadler?'

'I am *not*!'

'You are too, but I'm not going to argue with you about it.' He sighed and straightened up. 'So what's it to be, Catherine?' he asked. 'The cabin, the doctor—or what?' He waited, but she didn't reply. 'Catherine?'

'I don't know, Smitty,' she shook her head lightly, her voice nothing more than a whisper. 'I'll have to think about it.'

'On the offchance that you wanted the cabin Sadler's going ahead with contacting his friend.' Smitty paused, his expression growing wary. 'He's even offered to drive you up there first thing in the morning.'

'He's quite sure of himself, isn't he?' Somehow

Catherine managed to look mildly impressed. 'He makes one suggestion and bingo, it automatically becomes an order!'

'That's not true,' he groaned lightly. 'But if you should decide to take the cabin certain arrangements have to be made. What do you want me to tell him?'

'I still don't know,' she frowned. 'I'll have to think about it.'

'All right, Catherine,' he agreed reluctantly. 'Whenever you decide, you tell me.'

CHAPTER SIX

THE sun was a hot early morning orange glow on the horizon as Catherine stood by the window and watched it. She was up and dressed this morning, but she wasn't any closer to making a decision about the cabin than she had been last night. Something told her she would only know the answer to that after she had talked to Sadler.

She was certain of one thing, and that was that she couldn't continue to stay in bed any longer. Smitty's threat of calling in the doctor was too much of a real possibility for her to ignore. And while she didn't consider herself anywhere near the nervous breakdown stage—Sadler's medical opinion aside—she reluctantly admitted that she had to start living her life again. And if that meant fighting with Sadler . . . she sighed and squared her shoulders . . . well, so be it.

The doorbell to the apartment rang and she turned away from the window, her cool green gaze in steady anticipation of the knock on her door.

'It's Sadler, Cat.' He knocked and paused, an uncertain note in his voice. 'May I come in?'

'Of course, Sadler,' Catherine replied sweetly. 'The door's open. In fact,' she paused and smiled to herself, 'I've been waiting for you.'

'Oh?' Not knowing what to expect from her after a remark like that, Sadler opened the door and cautiously peered around the edge. His sharp grey gaze found the smiling Catherine immediately, but her hands were empty, so he shrugged and stepped in.

Dressed in jeans, brown boots and a lightweight baby-blue turtleneck sweater, he looked rugged, virile and—as always—completely sure of himself. But not of Catherine, if his warily narrowing eyes were any indication.

'I've got to hand it to you, Sadler,' she greeted him with those words and a big smile, 'that was a nice try.'

'What was?'

'Oh, don't be coy, it doesn't suit you.' She smiled and shook her head, the sunlight gently filtering through the window behind her, bathing her hair in a pale red-gold glow. 'You know exactly what I mean—nervous breakdown?—the doctor? I'm not that bad and you know it. I'm up, aren't I?' she gestured.

He conceded the point with a nod. She was up and dressed in jeans, sneakers and a red-checked blouse, but her complexion was as pale as yesterday.

'So why are you trying to get rid of me?' she demanded, the smile gone and her expression tightening. 'First the doctor and then the cabin in the woods. Your concern for my mental health is touching, but do I look that stupid, Sadler? You're up to something,' her eyes narrowed thoughtfully. 'I just haven't figured out what it is, and until I do, I'm not going anywhere.'

'Suit yourself, Cat,' he shrugged indifferently, tossing himself down on her bed, his long frame stretched out from head to toe. Clasping his hands under his head, he stared absently towards the ceiling, giving the impression of total indifference while all the time watching her carefully from the corner of his eye. 'I only mentioned the cabin to Smitty because I thought you might enjoy a few days away from everything. To be honest with you, Cat,' he paused, 'I think you need to get away.'

'Away from *you*, you mean,' she replied tightly.

'Have it your own way,' he shrugged, 'but as far as my trying to get rid of you is concerned, I'm the one,' he tapped his chest, 'who's been trying to get you to come into the office and lend a hand, or have you forgotten all those phone calls already? What did you think they were about? Maggie's a gem,' he continued, 'but she can't do it all by herself and she couldn't be expected to. It wouldn't hurt you to honour us with a personal appearance now and then. I've got a few things you could do to make yourself useful.'

'Like make your coffee?' Catherine muttered under her breath.

He lifted his head and looked at her. 'What?'

'Nothing.' She drew her lips together tightly and stared at him.

'Of course,' he continued with a lazy drawl, 'nobody is forcing you to do anything. If you want to you can crawl right back into bed and . . .'

'And have you find some quack to have me committed? No, thanks, Sadler,' she shook her head. He was up to something, but what? She couldn't go back to bed again—even Smitty had threatened to call the doctor about that. And she *wouldn't* go into the office—it was the principle of the thing now. Her expression narrowed thoughtfully; there didn't seem to be too many options open. Maybe she should get away for a while . . . 'How far is this cabin? And get your feet off my bed!'

'It's a good four-hour drive, maybe more.' Sadler sat up and put his feet on the floor. 'Don't tell me you're changing your mind—*again*?'

She glanced at his jeans and sweater. 'You're not planning on staying up there, too.' It was an order, not a question. 'Because if you are . . .'

'Me?' He looked surprised. 'I can't afford to take the time off, Cat.' He smiled pleasantly at her. 'One of us has to work.'

Catherine made a face and threw open the closet door. 'I'm entitled to a vacation,' she pulled down the suitcase from the shelf up over her head. 'I haven't had any time off in three years, except when I had the 'flu—and that doesn't count. I think a week or two in the mountains will do me some good.' She suddenly glanced at him. 'How long can I have the cabin?' she asked. 'Smitty didn't tell me.'

'For as long as you want it,' he replied, heading for the door. 'And as long as you have decided to go, do you think you can snap it up? It's a long drive up there, Cat, and another long drive back. I want to get back here early, I've got a dinner engagement for this evening.'

'This fast enough for you?' Catherine began throwing her clothes into the suitcase. 'I certainly wouldn't want to make you late for your date. Sophia, no doubt.' What she thought of that arrangement chinked like frozen ice crystals in her voice.

'That's right,' he nodded, lowering his lashes to hide the look that suddenly sprang to his eyes. 'We had a good time the other night, so I saw no reason not to do it again. Sophia's attractive,' he waxed lyrical, 'she's pleasant company and she's got a good sense of humour.'

'She'd have to have a *great* sense of humour to want to go out with you!' She slammed her suitcase closed and swung it off the bed. It was heavier than she had thought, and the momentum carried it—and her—crashing into the bedroom door as she tried to get through the doorway.

'Didn't you tell me that was a new door?' Sadler smiled innocently at her. 'Do you want me to carry that?'

'No,' she snapped. 'I want you to stand there all day talking about Sophia!' Her green eyes flashed when he didn't move right away. 'Well, you're the one who's in the big hurry . . . are we going to go or not?'

'We are *definitely* going to go.' Smiling to himself, Sadler followed her as she turned and started lugging her suitcase down the hallway towards the front door.

'Hey, Cat, wake up!' Sadler's voice was as gentle and soft as the touch of his hand on her shoulder. 'We're here!'

Catherine resisted. She was comfortable, warm and strangely contented. She didn't even remember falling asleep, all she had done was close her eyelids for just a moment and feel her head slip slowly towards Sadler's shoulder. 'Did I fall asleep?' It was a silly question under the circumstances, but one she needed to ask. It was the best sleep she'd had in weeks and she wanted to make sure it had really happened and wasn't something weird, as if she was beginning to daydream about sleeping.

'You fell asleep about two minutes after you got into the car.' Sadler's smile warmed as he looked at the sleepy-kitten expression on her face. 'That's not saying a whole lot for my company!'

Catherine stretched lazily and sat up straight, blinking her eyes until they agreed to stay open long enough for her to see where she was. 'Boy, you weren't kidding when you said it was isolated!' Her glance found nothing to look at but trees, trees and more trees. 'I can't even see the cabin. Where is it?'

Sadler squinted and glanced off through the trees to his left. 'There should be a path somewhere . . . yes, there it is,' he pointed. 'Bill said it was only a short walk from here.'

She looked surprised. 'You haven't been here before?'

'Uh-huh,' he shook his head no, his hand searching for something in his pockets. 'I don't have any idea what it's like. Bill's offered me the use of his cabin several times, but I've never taken him up on it.' He smiled as his hand finally located the object of his search. 'Here,' he handed her a lone key, 'unlock the door while I start to bring in some of this stuff.'

Nodding, she slid from the Jag and started up the path towards the still invisible cabin, her shoes making no sound on the soft spongy pine-needled ground. Not realising she was smiling, she stopped and listened to the forest, breathing deeply of the fresh pine-scented air around her. High in the trees a soft summer breeze rustled the leaves and directly up over her head, she grinned, sat a small grey squirrel, his scolding chatter and swishing tail telling her he was angry at having his quiet domain invaded.

The path led on to a small but comparatively tall building with the roof sharply sloped down on one side and a narrow, open porch across the front. Catherine had formed no preconceived idea about the cabin—the word 'cabin' was so innocuous—that when she unlocked the door and stepped inside she was immediately surprised—pleasantly so.

Basically, the entire cabin was only one large room. To her right as she looked into the cabin stood a massive native stone fireplace that acted as a room divider. On one side was the living-room and at the rear was what looked to be the kitchen. Over her head and to her left and extending about halfway over the living-room was a sleeping loft, the wide open balcony railing providing anyone up there a magnificent view of the first floor. The furniture was of simple design, but obviously comfortable; a large easy chair, a small table with a lamp, and facing the fireplace a long, tweedy-looking sofa—the perfect place to curl up at night to watch the flickering flames.

'Oh, Sadler!' She heard him on the porch behind her and turned towards him. 'It's perfect! I love it. It's got a loft,' she pointed, 'and a fireplace and everything. Oh, Sadler,' her delight made her bubble, 'I would have thought you would have been here before now—I know how you love the mountains.' Her enthusiasm began to fade slightly. 'Why haven't you been here before, or was it because you haven't been back to West Virginia lately?'

'That's part of it,' he shrugged as he glanced for the first time around the room, his gaze coming to rest on the solitary bed in the loft—king-sized, but still the only bed around. 'But basically the reason I haven't been here before now is that I haven't found . . .'

'I know,' she interrupted with a frown. It was the same

old excuse. 'You haven't found the *time*. That always was your problem, Sadler. You never could find the time.'

'No, Cat,' his grey eyes darkened, 'that's not what I was going to say. I've never been here before because I've never found anyone I wanted to bring up here with me.' His voice crisped, 'Understand?'

'Perfectly.' She thinned her lips. Of course Sadler wouldn't come up here without a little female companionship. But now that he knew what the cabin was like maybe Sophia would be the lucky one. Pushing the prickly thought aside, she wandered towards the kitchen. 'Sadler!' She came to a sudden halt and groaned. 'I don't have anything to eat,' her eyes widened with alarm as she faced him. 'Nothing. I didn't even think about bringing food.'

'I'm not surprised,' he arched a dark eye brow. 'You haven't thought about food in days. But I did.'

'You did what?'

'Thought about bringing along food—pay attention, Cat! I stopped off at the store before I picked you up this morning. It's in the back of the car.'

'You must have been certain I was going to agree to come up here,' her expression narrowed warily. She'd had the same thought last night.

'Not really,' he sighed loudly on purpose. 'No matter what you decided to do about the cabin the food wouldn't have gone to waste. I have to eat too, you know. I simply would have kept it. And before you get yourself all excited about that,' he continued calmly, 'the only reason I stopped before I picked you up was that I didn't want to take the chance of your wanting to stop off someplace on the way up here. Once you get into a store there's no getting you out!'

'Oh, that's right,' she smiled at him icely. 'I forgot you were in a big hurry to get back to Charleston.'

Sadler's returning smile was a beautiful thing to see. 'Yes, I am,' he agreed.

'Well then,' she pinched her lips together, 'I suppose I should thank you for driving me up here and let you get on your way.' He cocked his head and waited, an expectant tilt to one dark eyebrow. She narrowed her eyes to match her lips. 'Thank you!' she snapped.

'That wasn't the most gracious "thank you" I've ever heard,' he looked amused, 'but I'll take it. You're entirely welcome.'

He looked seriously for a moment as he glanced around the longer than wider kitchen. 'The stove and refrigerator both run off bottled gas,' he told her. 'I'll get them started for you before I leave. There's no electricity up here,' he added, 'but there's several kerosene lamps and I think Bill said there's a battery-operated lamp somewhere. You'll have to look for it.' He started towards the front door. 'Well, don't just stand there, Cat, give me a hand. There's a lot to carry in.'

'A lot to carry in' was an understatement, and Catherine stared with dismay at the two bags of groceries he put in her arms, and then at the three bags he carried in himself. 'You've got enough food here for an army,' she muttered, dogging his heels back down the path. 'How long did you tell him I was going to be here?'

'I didn't. It's yours for as long as you want it.' He glanced back over his shoulder. 'I thought I'd come up next weekend for you,' he paused. 'But far be it for *me* to tell *you* how long you're going to stay here. That's entirely up to you. If you're not ready to come back then, stay on for another week.'

Catherine gnawed lightly on her lower lip as she followed Sadler into the kitchen. For the first time since agreeing to come up here it was finally dawning on her that she was going to be up here *alone* for a week at least, and for a second the idea panicked her. 'Sadler, I . . .'

'What, Cat?' He slid his bags on the kitchen table and looked up at her. 'What do you want?'

'I . . .' Catherine frowned and ran the back of her

hand across her lightly flushed cheek. 'I don't have any wood for the fireplace. It's bound to be cool in the evenings and a little fire would feel good.'

'Oh?' If Sadler believed that the look on his face didn't reflect it. He stood leaning back slightly, pressing a shoulder against the back door as he stared across the kitchen at her. 'Bill said there was plenty of wood stacked right outside the back door.' He nodded obliquely in that direction. 'You should have more then enough wood, and if you don't . . .' he smiled, 'the woods are full of it.

'And that reminds me,' he bent down behind the refrigerator, his voice sounding muffled from the cramped quarters, 'there's a small pond over this way,' his pointing hand shot out, 'at least I think that's where it is. Ah well, you'll find it.' He stood up, dusted off his knees, brushed off his hands and looked as if he was ready to go. 'You're all set,' he informed her. 'Everything seems to be working. If you need to get a phone it's about three miles back down the road at a little general store—you can't miss it. And the road out in front is a dead end, so you shouldn't be bothered by anyone coming by.

'I almost envy you this week, Cat,' he sighed, and glanced around. 'You're not the only one who hasn't had any time off in a long time. Oh well,' he smiled suddenly, 'enough of that. I've got to get going, it's a long drive back.' He started to walk passed a very forlorn-looking Catherine when he suddenly stopped, looked at her as if he'd forgotten something, then cupped her chin gently in his hand and kissed her ever so softly on the mouth. ''Bye, Cat—be good!'

'Sadler!' Catherine grabbed his arm with both her hands. 'Sadler, don't . . .' But she never finished it. Her shoulders sagged and she released his arm, letting her hands fall back to her sides. 'Nothing,' she smiled, and shook her head. 'Goodbye.'

'What were you going to say, Cat?' Sadler's voice was

so soft and his presence so reassuring to her that she *almost* asked him to stay. Almost—but not quite.

'I . . . I was going to say,' she forced a smile, 'don't forget to come for me next weekend. I'd hate to have to walk home from here!'

'I won't.' His grey eyes seemed to see right through her. 'How could I ever forget you?' His voice suddenly changed and he smiled broadly. 'You'll be fine.' He gave her a reassuring pat on the rump and started for the door. 'You've got plenty to eat and nothing to do but rest and relax. And if you should need anything the store and the phone are just a nice hike away. Just don't buy more than you can carry for three miles.'

Catherine stayed on the porch and watched him walk down the narrow path towards his car, his long sure strides taking him farther and farther away, and with him went the last of her nerve. She didn't know what was the matter with her—normally she loved to be by herself, only right now just the thought of it terrified her. 'Sadler!' Her hand flew out as if to stop him. *'Sadler!'*

At the far end of the path Sadler caught the sound of her voice and turned, saw her wave and waved back. 'See you in a week,' he shouted. 'Take care of yourself!' and with that he was gone.

Hot tears were quick to sting Catherine's eyelids, and with only a second's hesitation she flew down the steps and ran quickly towards the car. But as fast as she thought she was, she wasn't quite quick enough, and when she got to the edge of the trees all she saw was the brightly coloured Jag start to pull away. But as a numbed Catherine watched a strange thing began to happen; the Jag sputtered, made a funny grating noise and then stopped dead in the middle of the road.

Out of breath from her sprint down the path, she stood by the side of a large tree and stared. 'What's the matter?'

'I'm not sure.' Sadler got out of his car and lifted the

hood, a worried look crossing his face as he peered down inside. 'It could be the battery,' he frowned, 'but that's brand new. It sounds more like the starter's shot, but I hope not.' He paused and did greasy little things with his fingers to the top part of the engine.

'Maybe you're out of gas?' she suggested, a familiar sharpness appearing in the tone of her voice.

'No, Cat,' he glanced out from under the hood, 'I'm not out of gas.'

'Then can you fix it?'

Sadler shut the hood and straightened up, taking his own sweet time before answering her. 'Not if it's the starter, I can't.' He glanced sourly down the road. 'I suppose I'll have to walk back to the store and try to locate a garage in the area that's equipped to fix the Jag. Although,' he frowned as he scanned the heavily wooded area around them, 'up here I don't think that's very likely.'

A moment ago Catherine had been on the verge of asking him to stay. No . . . she was going to *beg* him to stay or take her back with him, and now when it looked as if he might be staying, she perversely wanted the opposite. 'But you are going to try and find a garage, aren't you?' Her expression tightened. 'I mean, there must be someone *somewhere* who can fix it. All you've got to do is find it.'

Sadler caught the note in her voice—it would have been impossible not to—and his own expression hardened accordingly. 'Yes, *Catherine*,' he clipped, 'I just got through saying I was going to try. And I am—right now!' He reached inside his car and pulled out a rag. Wiping the grease from his hands, he glanced at his wrist watch, then at the sun. 'Depending on how much trouble I have finding a garage that can fix the Jag, I should be back in an hour or two.'

'An hour or two?' Her green eyes widened. 'You mean you're going to walk?'

'Unless you have a better suggestion?' He tossed the

rag on the floor of his car and then from the back withdrew a denim jacket.

'No,' she shrugged weakly, 'I guess not.'

'I'll be back as soon as I can, Cat.' Hooking his thumb in the collar of his jacket, he flipped it over his shoulder and left, leaving a sullen Catherine staring after him long after he had disappeared from her sight.

She stood in the centre of the tiny kitchen vaguely wondering why there wasn't any clock in the entire cabin. In her haste to pack, she frowned, she had forgotten to bring her watch, so she had no idea of the time. But it had to be getting on late afternoon. She peered out of the back-door window. The sun's rays were beginning to brush the tops of the trees, and while actual sunset was still a few hours away the shadows were starting to lengthen and in parts of the forest patches of night had already settled in. Surely Sadler had had enough time by now to walk to the store—wherever it was—find out if there was a garage in the vicinity that could fix his car, and walk back here to the cabin.

In the time he had been gone she had put the groceries away, which still seemed like an awful lot for one person, took a look around the cabin, fell in love with the view from the loft, and even had time to make a big salad and chill it.

She sat in the kitchen and waited, her foot beginning to tap nervously on the floor. Inadvertently it was her tapping foot that muffled the sound of footsteps on the porch outside the cabin. When the door opened and Sadler stepped in Catherine made no attempt to hide the relief in her eyes and in her voice. She'd been *so* worried! 'Hi!' She hurried to meet him. 'I was beginning to worry about you.'

A slightly dusty Sadler seemed amused and pleased by her choice of words. 'Worried, Cat?' He brushed the dust from his jacket sleeves. 'About me? That's a comforting thought.'

'You know what I mean,' she paused. 'It's starting to get dark and I . . .' She stopped and stared at him. Her face must be apple red if the grin on his face was any indication. 'Did you find someone to fix the car?' she snapped, angry at herself more than Sadler.

'Yes . . . and no,' he answered, his grey eyes raking her as he passed. 'I found a garage that can do the work, but they don't have the part in stock.'

'And *what* is that supposed to mean?' Catherine bored holes in his broad back as he walked over to the sofa and flopped down, his legs swinging up to dangle comfortably over the arm.

'It means, Cat,' flat on his back, he picked up his head, opened one eye and looked at her, 'that I'm not going anywhere—at least not for tonight. The garage are going to call around in the morning and see if they can locate a starter. If and when they do, they'll come out here with a tow-truck and take the car back to the garage to fix it.'

'Tomorrow is Saturday, Sadler,' she pointed out in not-so-gentle tones, her hand going to her hip in an angry gesture. 'And the day after that is *Sunday*. Most places like that are only open half a day on Saturday and not at all on Sunday.'

'I've already considered that, Cat,' he yawned, and put his head back down, 'but there's not a thing I can do about it. Brace yourself, darling,' his grey eyes seemed to smile at her even though they were closed, 'it may be Monday or Tuesday at the earliest before I can leave here.'

'But . . . but . . . but . . .' she stammered, her green eyes wide with alarm, 'that means you'll be here for *days!*'

'Believe me, Cat,' one eye opened again. 'I'm not any happier about this than you are. I had plans for this weekend . . . to work among other things.'

Catherine had a pretty good idea what his 'other things' were, and her lips thinned. 'Celibacy's good for your soul, Sadler,' she snapped, suddenly thinking of something vaguely connected. 'And that reminds me,' she paused, 'just where *are* you going to sleep? In case you hadn't noticed, there's only one bed in the loft and it's mine,' she tapped her chest. 'You're not sleeping there!'

'Well, I'm not sleeping in the Jag!' He sat up quickly, his claim to the bed as valid as hers.

'The bed is *mine*,' she hissed, reading his mind perfectly. 'And don't plan on sleeping with me, Sadler, because you're not!'

'Shouldn't you wait, dear, until you're asked?' he smirked, getting great pleasure of Catherine's suddenly pink cheeks. 'That particular thought never crossed my mind. I thought we'd draw straws for the bed.'

'Ha!' she snorted. 'You can forget that idea too.'

'Then *what* do you suggest?' he asked, sitting up sharply. 'I'm sure as hell not going to walk ten or twenty miles to find a hotel for the night just to pamper some perverted sense of modesty on your part.' He glanced down and patted the cushion next to him. 'It looks like I'll be sleeping right here.'

'If I didn't know better, Sadler,' Catherine's green eyes narrowed suspiciously, 'I'd say you had this all planned.'

'For what purpose, *Catherine*?' his voice hardened. 'I'm up to my eyeballs in that mess at Parker Plastics. In case you're interested,' he drawled the words sarcastically, 'the Internal Revenue Service called the other day. It seems there's a few questions about your last quarterly report. Would you care to make a comment?'

What Catherine made was a face and then she turned away. Sadler smiled and continued, 'I called Maggie from the store and explained the situation to her. She'll hold the fort until I get back.' He shrugged and sighed deeply, as if with keen disappointment. 'I won't even bother to mention the fact that my date with Sophia for this evening is ruined.'

'Good.' Catherine snapped irritably. 'Then *don't* mention it.'

As she turned the corner into the kitchen her expression mirrored her thoughts. On the surface everything Sadler had said made sense, and when you came right down to it, there wasn't any reason for her not to believe him. Maybe she was just getting paranoid when it came to Sadler. For now, she frowned lightly as she opened a cupboard door and removed two plates, she'd give him the benefit of the doubt. 'While I waited for you to come back,' she said partially over her shoulder, 'I made a salad. I thought you might be hungry, I know you didn't have any lunch.' She suddenly stopped talking and glanced into the other room. 'Or did you buy something to eat at the store?'

Sadler stood up, stretched and shook his head. 'No, I didn't.' He started walking towards the kitchen, his expression growing with appreciation at the sight of the salad on the table. 'That looks good, and I'm starved.' In the kitchen doorway he stopped, his eyes smiling slowly as he watched her fuss around the kitchen. 'You know what this reminds me of?'

'What?' Curious, Catherine glanced up.

'The forest?' he paused. 'You and your salad? All we need now is a nice mess of fish to fry and . . .'

'Our camping trip to Canada.' She remembered, and smiled. 'It's strange,' she mused, her expression reflective, 'that you should bring that up now. I was just thinking about that the other day.'

'Were you, Cat?' asked Sadler, his voice softened, and Catherine realised that she hadn't been the only one lately recalling their marriage. But after a four-year separation it would have impossible to meet again and *not* think about their marriage.

In the past few days she had relived almost every second of their marriage, but even now—after four years—the answer to one question still eluded her. 'What went wrong, Sadler?' Her question was whispered with uncertainty. She wanted to know the answer, yet she was fearful that the knowledge might bring more pain than understanding.

'In our marriage, Cat?' he asked slowly, his grey eyes sharply aware of her expression. 'I don't know how to answer that,' he shrugged. 'I don't know if there *is* an answer. I knew what went wrong four years ago—you did. No—let me finish,' he held up his hand when he saw her start to reply. 'You've asked the one question I've asked myself a hundred times lately, so let me see if I can find an answer for it. I think in order to do that,' he paused, 'we have to begin at the end.'

'The day you told me you were leaving me and filing for a divorce, Cat,' his voice was incredibly low, 'was the worst day of my entire life. I alternated between wanting to wring your neck and never wanting to see you again. Obviously I opted for the latter.'

'And I thought it was because you didn't care,' Catherine's green eyes filled with pain. 'You just turned around and walked out of my life, Sadler. And for four years I never saw you . . . not until that day in the restaurant.'

'It wasn't because I didn't care, Cat,' his white knuckles betrayed his softly spoken voice. 'I think I cared too much. That was only partly a joke about wanting to strangle you because I was afraid I *would* lose my temper with you, and I didn't want to do that. So I went away,' he sighed. 'I was hoping that with enough time and distance on my side I'd learn to get over you, but four years is a long time to wait. And what made it worse,' he continued, his voice stiffening slightly, 'was that I never fully understood what our problem was—not really. And I can't help but believe that we could have worked it out . . . if only you'd been willing to try.'

'But I'd *been* trying, Sadler,' Catherine's voice broke and she swallowed hard at the lump in her throat. 'But no matter how long or how hard I tried, I couldn't make myself get used to all the other women in your life—and don't look at me like that,' she thinned her lips. 'I'm not crazy. I know what I saw—the secret looks, the hidden glances from under their lashes when they thought I wasn't looking. Maybe I could have endured all that,' she gestured weakly, 'if it wasn't for the day in Argentina when I walked into your study and found you with Teresa in your arms. Teresa!' she spat the word. 'If you didn't care any more about me or our marriage than to carry on like that in our house . . .'

'Carry on like *what*?' Sadler's grey eyes were wide with surprise. 'I don't even remember the incident. What was I doing?'

'Oh, *please*!' Catherine sneered. 'What do you think you were doing?'

'I don't know.' His expression hardened. 'That's why I'm asking you.'

'You were kissing her!' she hissed, her eyes flaring. 'At least, that's what you were doing when I saw you. What happened after I left I wouldn't care to guess.'

'Oh . . .' Sadler nodded slowly, his gesture one of understanding and anger. 'Now I remember what you're talking about. But you should have stuck around, Cat,' his voice tightened. 'You walked out before the best part.'

Angry, Catherine started to do just that again, but he saw what she had in mind and grabbed her wrist, pulling her down into the nearest chair. 'Oh no, you don't,' he growled at her. 'You're not running out again. You started this and you're going to finish it.' His grip tightened on her wrist. 'If you'd only waited a few more seconds, my pet, you would have seen her leave. You're right as far as it goes, she *was* kissing me—or trying to. It's not only hard trying to kiss someone who's not interested, it's humiliating, and you would have seen that for yourself if your snooping had lasted a few more seconds.'

'But you . . . but she . . .' Catherine was struggling to keep the anger in her voice, but it wasn't easy when Sadler was telling her something she thought she already knew. 'Teresa wasn't the only one,' she tried to fight back. 'There were others.'

'No, Cat.' His lips tightened angrily. 'There were no other women. None. Not while I was married to you. Any affair I ever had was conducted solely in your imagination and solely for your own benefit—certainly not for mine. And as far as all those come-hither looks were concerned, did you ever see me return one? No!' he answered his own question. 'And you never would have. Why would I want any other woman when I had you?'

He stood back and stared at her for a moment. 'Maybe woman is the wrong word to use, Cat. A woman wouldn't have sat back and let another woman come into her house and try and take it over.'

'Teresa?' Catherine's eyes widened with surprise. 'You knew that was what she was doing? Then why didn't you say something to her? Unless . . .' her voice faded, 'unless that was what you wanted.'

'What I wanted,' his lips thinned, 'was a marriage. I knew ours was in trouble, but I thought if you got mad enough you'd fight back. But you didn't, Cat. You ran. So you see,' suddenly he looked and sounded very tired, 'while you were the only *female* in my life you weren't yet a woman. I needed a wife—what I got was a child bride who didn't need a husband as much as she needed a babysitter.'

'If that was the way you felt, Sadler,' Catherine chocked back hot tears, 'then why did you marry me in the first place?'

'Because I loved you, Catherine.' He stood very straight, very tall, and very remote. 'What man wouldn't? You were an appealing combination—half woman, half child. Just out of pigtails and braces but feeling the emotions and desires of a woman. I knew I was taking a chance, I just didn't realise how big a chance it was.'

'Then there were never any other women, not even

Teresa?' Catherine had such a sickening premonition of what his answer was going to be that she could barely get the words out.

'No, Cat.' Sadler was strangely unemotional and remote as he replied. 'There was never anyone but you.'

Her slim hand trembled as she put it to her burning cheek. 'Why . . . why didn't you tell me all this then?'

'When did you ever give me the damn chance?' His jaw tensed from a surge of unexpressed anger. 'One day we were married and the next day we weren't. And even if I had told you all that at the time,' he smiled bitterly, 'would you have believed me?'

'No.' Catherine was forced to be truthful with him no matter how much it hurt. 'No, I probably wouldn't have.'

'So . . .' he sighed, 'that's that. And to answer your question of what went wrong—I still don't know. Everything, maybe,' he shrugged. 'Maybe nothing. It doesn't matter now anyway, does it?'

'No,' she admitted, sick to her stomach, 'it doesn't matter now.'

Sadler's hands were clenched in powerful white-knuckled fists at his sides. Slowly he turned and started walking away from her.

'Where are you going?' she asked in a small voice.

'Out.' He kept walking away from her, his proud dark head rigid on his broad shoulders. 'I suddenly feel the need for some fresh air, Cat.'

'But . . . my,' she pointed a trembling finger towards the bowl on the table, '. . . my salad.''

'Eat it yourself. I'm not hungry.' He stopped when he reached the front door, his eyes frozen chips of grey steel as he turned to face her. 'And if you have any thoughts about waiting up for me, don't bother. I don't know when, or if, I'll be back.'

The sun had long since set for the night, leaving in Catherine a coldness she couldn't shake. With a weary sigh she finally gave up waiting for Sadler, put a blanket, a sheet and a pillow on the sofa for him, and then in the darkness started up the spiral staircase to the loft, her softly muffled footsteps echoing sadly behind her.

There was a skylight in the roof directly over the bed which provided a magnificent view of the star-filled heavens, but Catherine's wide-eyed stare appreciated very little of the blue-black velvet beauty.

She had no idea how long she lay there staring into the darkness, listening only to the sound of her heart, but finally the front door opened and Sadler came in. In the quiet she could hear him settle down for the night on the sofa, and only when all was quiet again did she close her eyes and finally fall asleep.

CHAPTER SEVEN

CATHERINE awoke the next morning to the faint aroma of freshly perking coffee in the air. It had to be Sadler, of course, and pushing aside the covers, she slid out of bed and walked silently to the edge of the balcony and looked over the railing. From her elevated position she could see directly into the kitchen, but one quick glance told her Sadler wasn't in the kitchen—he was sitting in a straight-backed wooden chair next to the cold fireplace, his long legs crossed at the ankles and up on the corner of the end table next to the sofa, his eyes aimed directly on her. 'Oh.'

'Good morning.' Sadler's unemotional greeting was just that—a polite greeting, nothing more, nothing less.

Catherine forced a smile. Not that she didn't want to smile, because she did, but because she was so suddenly tense that her face refused to obey her command. She had done a considerable amount of thinking last night while she was waiting for Sadler to come back, and all that thinking had produced at least one conclusion: she was not going to argue with him any more, at least not about their marriage. It wasn't his fault his car had broken down when it had, and as far as whose fault it was that their marriage failed . . . well, she frowned softly to herself, the less said about that the better. 'Is that coffee I smell?'

'It is,' he nodded, his expression still coolly noncommittal. 'It's just about through perking. Are you ready for a cup?'

'I'd love one.' Catherine's smile softened and became real. 'Give me two minutes to get dressed and I'll be right down.' She hurried, but it ultimately took her a little longer than two minutes, for she stood there worrying about her pale complexion in the bathroom mirror. After trying several hair-styles she finally settled on brushing it back and pinning it loosely to the back of her head, letting soft wispy tendrils frame her face and distract somewhat from the tired, hollow look around her eyes. Stuffing her nervous hands inside her jeans pockets, she walked into the kitchen. 'Sadler?'

'What, Cat?' He had just poured them both a cup of coffee and turned to put them on the table.

'I . . . I'm sorry about last night.' Her gaze fell to the floor at his feet, but in so doing she missed the expression on his face. 'I know you're not to blame because your car chose this particular time to break down, and I certainly shouldn't have dug all that up about our marriage. It's ancient history, all over and done with,' she gestured, 'and nothing we can say now will change one minute of it.'

That said, she forced herself to meet his eyes. 'As long as we're going to be together for a while can't we try to get along? I know I will. OK?'

'OK,' he nodded, looking strangely relieved as he sat down. 'As long as we avoid certain subjects we should be all right.' He looked thoughtful for a moment, his grey eyes on the verge of a smile. 'I guess that leaves us the weather and . . . the weather.'

Catherine's giggle was part relief, part amusement. 'Are we really as bad as all that?'

'Just about.' His frown was real and his dark brows nearly touched. 'But I agree—we both have to make an effort to get along for the next few days, or however long it should take to get the car fixed—for the sake of my ulcer,' he added, 'if nothing else.'

'Ulcer?' Catherine's worried glance skimmed the rim of her cup. 'I didn't know you had an ulcer. That's strange,' she frowned, 'you never impressed me as getting overly upset about anything. You always took things in your stride. Nothing ever bothered you,

Sadler,' her voice softened reflectively for a moment. 'I was always the one who blew up.'

'Just because I didn't shout and throw things, Cat, it didn't mean I wasn't upset.' Sadler's voice was very low, his words slowly spoken. 'Lots of things bother me. *You*, for instance—you bother me.' He suddenly grinned and sat back in his chair. 'But I think we're getting on to dangerous ground, so let's change the subject. No, I don't have an ulcer,' he shook his head, 'but I soon will have if I don't get something to eat—and soon! Do you realise I haven't had anything to eat since breakfast yesterday?' He stood up, opened the refrigerator door and peered inside. 'How does juice, bacon, eggs and pancakes sound?'

'It sounds like an awful lot,' Catherine's eyes widened, 'but I'll give it a try.' She was beginning to get her appetite back and she wasn't going to fight it—or Sadler. 'I'll start the bacon if you'll mix the pancakes.'

As she watched him walk around the kitchen in search of bowl and spoon, she was overwhelmed by a sense of incredible loss. If they had only had last night's conversation four years ago . . . But that would have been impossible, she sighed. Sadler was right—four years ago she wouldn't have listened to him. She'd been too filled with herself, Her wounded pride, her need for attention, her unreasonable fits of jealousy.

And it had been unreasonable, she knew that now, but a little voice inside her had told her last night that she'd known that all along. She hadn't spent the last four years trying to rid herself of Sadler's memory, she had spent all that time refusing to accept a large share of the blame. It wasn't hate that she felt when she thought of Sadler—it was guilt, guilt and waste. Four years wasted, gone for ever. Four years of her life spent hating the one man she'd ever loved. The one man she still loved.

Her heart flipped at the enormity of what she had just admitted to herself. She did still love Sadler, and as much as she ever had.

'Hey!' He looked at her from across the table. 'Just because our topics of safe conversation are severely limited that doesn't mean we can't talk at all! You're staring at your plate—did I burn the pancakes?'

'No, they're fine.' Pink-cheeked, Catherine smiled and shook her head. 'How are the eggs?'

'They're fine,' he nodded, a curious slant to his eyes. 'Just the way I like them.'

As his eyes met hers from across the table, she had the sudden feeling that he was reading her mind. Did he know she still loved him? Impossible, of course, but she couldn't stop her cheeks from burning anyway.

'That makes two,' he told her with a short nod.

'What does?' Confused, she glanced up.

'Two subjects,' he replied with an easy smile and the right amount of fingers. 'Food and the weather. We're moving right along!'

'Oh!' Catherine's returning smile was automatic, more of a reflex than a genuine response. He hadn't been thinking of her *or* reading her mind—he'd been thinking about food! 'Yes,' she agreed, 'I guess that makes two.'

She began to eat, and as she did she missed the strange look that crossed Sadler's face, which was probably just as well. If she had seen it, she would have recognised it, because it was a look she'd had a lot on her face the past four years—the look of guilt and regret.

'Catherine?' His voice sounded hollow and she glanced up quickly. He only called her Catherine when he was angry with her or when he was going to tell her something she didn't want to hear.

Instinctively she held her breath. 'What, Sadler?'

He hesitated, uncharacteristically running his fingers through the front of his thick black hair. 'Cat, I . . .' His gaze met hers and he stopped. Then he shook his head and smiled, 'I'm out of coffee—how about a refill?'

'Sure.' Her sigh of relief was audible. 'You perked it, so I'll pour it. I was just thinking the same thing myself.'

Sadler waited until she had returned to her chair before he spoke again, and when he did his voice was back to normal. 'When I get through with breakfast,' he told her, 'I'm going to split some of that wood in back of the cabin for Bill. I think it's the least I can do for the loan of his cabin *and* some of his clothes.'

'His clothes?' Catherine looked with a new appreciation of what he had on, noticing that he wasn't wearing the turtleneck sweater of yesterday but had on instead a red plaid shirt. 'Isn't that yours?'

'No,' he shook his head. 'This is Bill's. It's lucky for me he left a few things hanging in one of the closets, otherwise I'd be living in what I had on my back.'

'Really?' Catherine's delicate brow wrinkled into a puzzled frown. While she had waited for Sadler to return yesterday from trying to locate a garage she had been on a curiosity inspection of the cabin and didn't recall seeing any clothes hanging in either closet; the one upstairs next to the bathroom or the one down here next to the front door. 'That's lucky, all right.' Her voice faded softly. 'Especially when you consider he must be the same size you are. I remember having a hard time finding shirts right off the rack that fitted you, what with your long arms and wide shoulders, but that shirt's a perfect fit. If I didn't know better, Sadler,' she paused, her eyes narrowing slightly, 'I'd say that shirt was tailored for you.' Her voice tightened ever so slightly. 'Are those his slacks, too?'

Sadler stood up and lowered his thick black lashes as he glanced down at the neatly pressed navy coloured slacks. 'Yes. They fit pretty good, too, eh?'

'Better than "pretty good".' She stared at his legs. 'I'd say that was a perfect fit, too.'

'No, not really,' he disagreed with a shrug. 'The waist is a little tight.' He slid his thumb under the waistband and sucked in his stomach as if to prove his point. 'Bill must be a few pounds lighter than I am.' The sartorial inspection over, he grabbed his cup of coffee and started for the back door. 'I'll be right out here in the back if you want me.'

'Sadler?'

Catherine's voice stopped him dead in his tracks, his hand still on the doorknob. Every muscle in his body seemed to tense as he turned his head slowly to look at her. 'What, Cat?'

Catherine had begun to clear the dishes from the table and spoke to him half over her shoulder. 'Do you think they'll be able to fix the car today?'

'An honest appraisal, Cat?' he replied with a sigh of relief so loud as to be obvious, but Catherine missed it through the sudden clink of dishes in the sink. 'Or do you want me to tell you something you want to hear?'

'No,' she shook her head and turned to face him, her hands curling over the edge of the sink as if to brace herself, 'I want you to tell me what you think is really going to happen.'

'All right,' his grey eyes darkened. 'Then I doubt it. I'll consider myself lucky if I can get it fixed before some time late Monday, and even that's being optimistic. Tuesday would be a better guess.' He paused and looked at her, her expression becoming unreadable as she turned and stared into the sink. 'Is it going to be that much of a problem?' his voice softened, 'our being here together for a few days?'

'No, Sadler,' she smiled as she looked at him, 'it won't be a problem, at least not for me. I'm glad the car broke down, and I hope it won't be fixed for several days.'

'Why, Cat . . .' Sadler's eyes widened with pleasure, as did his smile. 'That's quite an admission—especially coming from you!'

'I know,' she laughed selfconsciously, ridiculously pleased with herself and the way she felt. 'And as long as I'm making all these wild confessions,' she hesitated slightly, 'I might as well go the whole way and tell you I wasn't waving you off yesterday. I wanted you to stop and come back. I . . .' her voice broke, 'I didn't want you to leave.'

Before Sadler had the chance to reply to her confession she felt her cheeks burn and began to laugh. 'How's that for honesty?' She turned her face to hide her hot cheeks. 'I . . . want us to get along while we're here, and I think that means being honest with one another.'

'Yes, Cat,' Sadler frowned and quickly turned away, a curiously troubled expression crossing his face, 'honesty is always important.'

The sun felt warm on Catherine's body as she stretched out lazily in a sunny patch on the soft ground. With her head propped up at a strange angle against the trunk of a tree, she peered through her pale lashes at Sadler, watching with a quiet fascination the way his muscles rippled powerfully beneath his glistening skin. He had worked up quite a sweat as he split wood and had to hang his shirt on a branchy bush next to her. As soon as he did she found it impossible to take her eyes off him.

As near as she could tell—and her memory was still incredibly sharp when it came to recalling Sadler—he hadn't lost or gained an ounce during their four-year separation. Any changes in him, what few there were, were superficial . . . like the distinguished silver streaks above his ears and perhaps a few more lines around the corners of his eyes. Sadler McQuade had changed very little, as had Catherine's feelings for him. He had the same unsettling effect on her now that he had had four years ago.

He swung the axe one final time in a wide arc over his head, splitting the last chunk of wood easily and leaving the blade jammed solidly into the splitting block. He straightened up slowly and faced Catherine, the damp coal-black hair on his chest curling tightly and tumbling downward until it disappeared seductively in the waistband of his slacks. His dark eyebrows arched slowly in an expression of growing amusement until Catherine realised, with burning cheeks, that while she'd been staring at him, he'd been talking to her.

'I'm sorry, Sadler,' her hand flew to cover her flushed cheeks, an action she tried to disguise by pretending to block the sun from her eyes. 'Did you say something?'

'I did,' he grinned, 'but you were a million miles away. What were you thinking about?'

She didn't answer as she quickly stood up, paying an intense interest to the few pine needles that were clinging to her jeans. 'I don't remember.' Her expression almost back to normal, she risked a quick glance at him. 'What did you say?'

'I said,' he grinned, 'that I thought you came out here to help me split wood?'

'I am!' she tried to look indignant. 'I'm giving you moral support. That's as important as actual physical labour.'

'Is it? I'll have to remember that.' He ran his handkerchief across his sweaty brow. 'While I appreciate all this moral support, how about something a little more substantial, like a cold drink?' he hinted, squinting up at the sun. 'I think I've been out here all morning.'

Catherine agreed with a quick nod. 'There's no soda,' she shook her head, 'but how does a glass of lemonade sound? I saw that you'd bought some of that powdered stuff when I put the groceries away.'

'That'll do, thanks,' he nodded. 'Just as long as it's good and cold.'

She put ice cubes in two glasses and opened the lemonade, but only half her mind was on the project. The other half was mulling something over that Sadler had said earlier in the morning. And oddly enough the sight of his shirt lying across the bush next to her had brought it all back. But why? Why did the innocent sight of that shirt bring a heavy uneasiness to her mind? Was it because she didn't remember seeing any clothes in either closet? Was Smitty right . . . was she really on the verge of a breakdown of some kind?

A sudden chill went down her spine, and leaving the glasses on the kitchen table a freshly worried she walked reluctantly into the other room and over to the closet by the front door. Fearful of what she would find, she held her breath and slowly opened the door. Hanging in what she would have sworn had been an empty closet were several shirts, another turtleneck sweater that was definitely Sadler's style, a lightweight summer jacket, and a couple of pairs of jeans—all of which looked in remarkably good shape to be something to be left hanging in a seldom used cabin.

For a moment Catherine stood staring into the closet, her finger lightly across her tightly drawn lips. Something about all this just didn't feel right to her, but this wasn't the time to delve into it, for either of the two possibilities that sprang to mind were unacceptable to her. She was either losing her memory and maybe her mind, *or* for some unknown reason Sadler was lying about the clothes.

Catherine shook her head violently, dismissing that idea as quickly as she could. For the first time in over four years she and Sadler had established a working relationship. It wasn't the relationship they had had when they were first married—that was impossible now—but at least they were talking *to* instead of shouting *at* one another, and Catherine didn't want anything to spoil it.

'Hey!' Sadler's shout came from outside the back door. 'How long does it take to mix up a little powdered lemonade? I'm about to die of thirst out here!'

'I'm coming!' Pushing her unsettling thoughts and paranoid misgivings out of her mind, Catherine picked up the two glasses from the kitchen table and hurried outside to join him.

Outside the cabin night had fallen, settling down with the total pitch blackness that can only happen in the mountains where there are no city lights to soften the darkness. Inside the cabin, however, was a darkness of a different kind—softly flickering shadows, warm cosy feelings . . . mellow at its best.

Catherine sat on one end of the sofa, her legs tucked up under her, her head resting against the back. There was a lazy warmth emanating from the roaring flames in the fireplace, and her heavy eyelids seemed determined to stay closed in spite of her valiant efforts to the contrary.

'Are you asleep?' Sadler's question floated over to her from his end of the sofa. 'I thought we were here to play checkers? If I recall, you were the one who demanded the chance to get even.'

'I do.' Her eyelids fluttered open, Sadler's fuzzy image bringing a smile to her lips. 'And we will. I only shut my eyes for just a minute. I was concentrating.'

'Uh-huh,' he agreed with a grin. 'And the snoring? What about that—or is that concentrating too?'

'I never!' Her eyes flew open wide, the yellow-orange firelight reflecting like flashing green flames in her large night-time pupils. Ready to defend her sleeping habits, she saw Sadler's teasing expression and laughed, her smile staying on her lips long after the laugh had died down. She had been smiling a lot these past two days; with just the two of them here in the cabin it seemed natural, and the smile on her face was almost permanent.

'I'm glad you split all that wood yesterday,' she glanced over her shoulder towards the fire. 'After being so warm yesterday, it's hard to believe today would turn so cold and rainy.' She hesitated only briefly. 'Do you think it will rain again tomorrow?'

'I don't know, Cat.' Sadler didn't look at her, but continued to stare at the dark amber liquid in the glass in his hand. 'You know the mountains—you can never be sure what it's going to do.'

Catherine nibbled gently on a fingernail, the mention of tomorrow bringing more to her mind than the weather. Tomorrow was Monday, and since they hadn't heard from the garage that they had found the part necessary to fix the car, there was a good chance that they would get that news tomorrow. And with the car repaired Sadler would have no reason to stay—and every reason to leave. She sighed deeply, realising that in spite of the bad start to the weekend, she was reluctant now to see it come to an end.

'Why the big sigh?' Sadler asked softly, his features deeply etched by the firelight, his eyes reflecting diamond-shaped specks of light in the darkness. 'What were you thinking??'

'About tomorrow,' she replied truthfully. 'I . . . I've been thinking, Sadler . . . if they can fix the car tomorrow I'll go back with you.' Her gaze travelled wistfully around the cabin. 'I don't want to stay here any more.'

'You don't?' He was surprised. 'Why not? I thought you liked it up here?'

'I do, very much,' she paused. 'But . . . well, it won't be the same up here by myself. I might as well go back with you and give Maggie a hand at the office. It's not fair of me to expect her to do it all. It's my responsibility, not hers.'

Instead of being pleased by her news, Sadler looked upset, almost angry. 'Does that mean you're planning on going into the office everyday?'

'Yes,' she nodded slowly. 'I've been childish about that and I know it. Facts are facts, Sadler,' her smile looked sad in the firelight. 'I couldn't handle Parker's and you can. It's as simple as that,' she shrugged.

His expression was dark, moody—not an expression that came easily to his features. 'You didn't do that badly, Cat,' his voice was incredibly low. 'You had the mess dumped in your lap and in the circumstances you did a damn good job just to keep it afloat as long as you did.'

'Really?' That admission, coming from Sadler, was

high praise indeed, and Catherine literally beamed. 'I didn't do that badly?' she echoed.

'You did good, Cat,' he smiled. 'Very good.'

Basking in the warmth of Sadler's praise, she smiled contentedly as she readjusted the blanket around her legs. She felt wonderful, relaxed and comfortable with Sadler around, sitting like this and talking—or not talking—it didn't matter, just as long as he was there. She closed her eyes and snuggled up against the sofa, surprising no one when she immediately fell asleep.

She was more asleep then awake when she felt Sadler slip his arms under her and pick her up. 'I thought you wanted to play checkers?' he asked, his breath a soft tickle across her forehead.

'We still can,' she protested weakly. 'Put me back down.'

'And watch you sleep?' he grinned. 'No, thanks. I've been doing that for the past hour or so, and as lovely as you are to look at I'm beginning to get tired myself.' He adjusted her weight in his arms and began walking towards the spiral staircase that led to the loft. 'And since we were sitting on what amounts to my bed,' he continued with a smile, 'I can't go to sleep until you go to bed. See?'

Catherine did, very clearly, and came up with what she thought was the perfect solution. 'Then sleep with me,' she whispered.

He caught himself from stumbling just in time. 'That wasn't a hint on my part, Cat,' he shook his head soberly.

'I know that,' she nodded, 'but the offer still stands.'

'You don't know what you're talking about.'

'Yes, I do.' She clung to his neck sleepily, her eyes barely open. 'That sofa is too small for you and you know it. I woke up last night and peeped over the railing at you. Your bare feet were hanging off one end and your neck was all bent out of shape on the other end. I've got this huge, big king-size bed up here and I don't use a quarter of it. You can have the other half.'

'I think not,' he smiled softly at her. 'Your offer is generous and for that I thank you, but it's not very practical.' He came to a halt at the edge of the bed and began to lower her on to it. Instinctively she tightened her grip around his neck, forcing him to bend down over the bed with her.

'Your offer's tempting, Cat,' he admitted, brushing a quick, light kiss across her sleepy lips. 'You'll never know *how* tempting, but look at you,' he unwrapped her arms from his neck and stood up. 'You're half asleep now.'

'No, I'm not,' she protested, trying to sit up and keep her eyes open at the same time. It wasn't easy. 'See!'

'Go to sleep,' he laughed gently. 'I'll see you in the morning.'

In the dim light, Catherine watched him reluctantly make his way down the stairs. 'Reluctant' was the word her sleepy version gave to the way he suddenly stopped halfway down the stairs, turned and looked at her from across the floor. It was only a brief look and even at that it was partially hidden by the shadows in the stairway, but Catherine saw it—and felt it. Sadler didn't want to leave her, he didn't want to, but he did, and with a deep sigh he continued down the stairs to the sofa below.

Sitting on the edge of the bed, she listened as he put more wood on the fire and settled down for the night. Slipping on her nightgown, she walked silently to the railing and looked down, expecting to find him stretched out on the sofa below. He wasn't—he was still fully clothed and sitting motionless in the centre of the sofa, his arms outstretched on either side of him, his gaze aimed stonily into the dancing flames. Shivering from the sudden cold, she pulled her arms around herself and hurried back to bed.

An hour later a once sleepy Catherine now lay wide awake and restless. It was hard to believe that just a short time ago she had been so tired she could hardly keep her eyes open, and now it was just the opposite; she was so wide awake she couldn't keep them shut.

Sleep stubbornly refused to come to her no matter what she did or how much she tossed and turned. And she knew why. Everything had been so perfect these past few days that it was only natural for her to think of Sadler in more affectionate terms. Affection equals love equals making love, and Sadler was the only man she had ever known. He was her first lover and he was still her only lover.

Shivering from nerves now more than cold, Catherine crept from her bed and tiptoed over to the railing. The fire had long since died down to hot ashes, supplying very little light and even less heat. Sadler sat on the sofa in exactly the same position as before. He hadn't moved at all.

'Sadler?' Catherine's voice was soft and strangely breathless, but he heard her, she knew he did, because even from that distance she felt him tense.

'What is it, Cat?' his voice sounded tired.

'I . . .' She swallowed the lump in her throat. 'I can't sleep, Sadler.'

'Well, that makes two of us,' he sighed. 'Do you want some warm milk?'

'No,' she shook her head. She didn't want warm milk.

'Then I'm fresh out of suggestions,' he sighed again, his gaze still locked on the dying ashes in the fireplace. 'I can't seem to get myself to sleep tonight, so I don't know what I can do for you. Go on back to bed and try it again.'

Catherine pressed her hands tightly together as she stared down at him. She wanted to try it again, she wanted her and Sadler to try it again. Intellectually she realised time and distance had separated them, but emotionally virtually nothing had changed for her. 'Sadler?'

'*What*, Catherine?' His voice had a little edge to it.

'Come to bed.' Her suggestion was out before she

realised it, and her breath caught in her throat as she waited for his reply.

'We've been through all that before, Cat,' he replied, finally standing up to look at her. Legs slightly apart, his arms folded across his chest, he seemed to look right through her. 'In fact,' he paused, 'I think we've been through all this a *couple* of times before.'

'A couple of times?' she whispered, recalling only one—her innocent invitation to share her bed tonight. 'I don't . . .' eyes wide, she stared. 'You don't mean that night in my apartment? But this isn't the same thing, Sadler. You can't compare them.'

'It isn't?' His voice sounded hard.

'No! That was different,' she shook her head, her cheeks burning from the memory.

'Why?' he demanded. 'Why was it different?'

'Why?' she echoed weakly. 'Well, because . . . because . . .'

'Because you didn't mean it? Because you wanted something from me then and now you don't?' Sadler's suggestions sounded like accusations to her.

'I'm not sure,' she whispered, because there was a certain amount of truth in what he said. She *did* want something from him—she wanted him to make the last four years go away. But nothing or no one could do that for her now. 'Never mind, Sadler,' she gulped at what threatened to a sob. 'It doesn't matter now.' Her hand pressed tightly to her lips, she turned and ran towards her bed, throwing herself miserably across the top of it. Was she forever destined to make a fool of herself over Sadler?

Her sobs, as quiet as they were, were loud enough to muffle the sound of footsteps on the spiral staircase leading to the loft. It was ultimately Sadler's presence next to the bed that made her look up, and not any noise. 'Go away, Sadler,' she quickly wiped her eyes with the back of her hand.

'No.' Sadler stood next to the bed, his eyes so dark a

grey they looked black in the fading light. 'You don't want me to go—not really.'

'Yes, I do!' Catherine started to sit up. She really believed what she was saying, and her eyes widened with determination.

'You don't know what you want, Cat. You never did.' He sat down next to her on the bed. 'That's always been your problem, and up to now I've always sat back and let you try to work it out yourself. But not this time, Cat. This is too important to both of us.' He reached for her in the darkness, his hands coming to rest on the front of her nightgown. 'This is one decision that's going to be made for you.'

Catherine started to protest, she even put up her hand to stop him, but the protest died on her lips as soon as she touched him.

'You knew this was inevitable, Cat,' his whispered husky words sent shivers down her spine. 'It had to happen . . . it was just a matter of time.' Her nightgown had twisted itself around her, and as he moved his hand across her body he became entangled in one of the folds. With a soft growl he gave a tug, only instead of freeing the gown he tore it slightly. He paused, took a deep breath and finished ripping it off, throwing it indifferently towards the foot of the bed.

Catherine clutched the sheet across her body, her nerves quickening with anticipation as she watched him unbutton his shirt. 'I'm scared, Sadler,' she whispered, watching his shirt slip off his back and fall to the floor.

'Scared?' He stopped undressing and looked at her, his expression hidden in the shadows. 'Of me? I'm not going to hurt you. That nightgown was . . .'

'No, no,' she shook her head, 'it's not that. It's . . .' She paused, her body trembling. 'This is silly,' she admitted, trying to scold herself out of the feeling, 'but it's almost like the first time all over again. And in a way . . .' her voice faded until Sadler could barely hear it, 'I guess it is.'

He was next to her now, his body so close she could feel the warmth from his skin on hers. 'There hasn't been anyone since you, Sadler,' she whispered. 'You're still the only one.'

His body tensed, his grip on her waist tightening noticeably. 'No one, Cat,' he repeated in uncertain tones. 'Not once in all those years?'

'No one, Sadler.' Her heart raced so fast it was all she could do to get the words out. In all that time she hadn't met anyone she wanted to share the ultimate intimacy with—no one but Sadler. Every man she had ever met fell far short by comparison and she hadn't realised, until just now, that she *had* been comparing them to Sadler. 'I guess,' she whispered, her body coming alive from his touch, 'that you've spoiled me for anyone else.'

'Oh, Cat,' he sighed, drawing her body towards him and moulding her supple willing body into his, 'I wish I could tell you I've been a monk these past few years, but I can't. There were a few women, but they were just *there* for me. Can you understand?' He buried his face in the hollow of her throat, drawing deeply of the sensual, mystical scent of her body. 'They weren't you.'

His lips burned her as he left a trail of kisses from her breast to her mouth, finally claiming her lips with an urgency that surprised her. Caught up in the present, Catherine finally let go of the past and for the first time in her life she didn't care about other women—real or imagined. She had Sadler, and as her arms slid across his shoulders she realised that Sadler was all she ever really wanted.

CHAPTER EIGHT

'GOOD morning.'

Catherine's eyelids were still heavy with sleep when she heard Sadler's husky early morning voice, and smiling slowly to herself she snuggled up closer to him. 'If that's a question,' she purred lazily, her green eyes still sparkling with a contented glow, 'then the answer's yes, it *is* a good morning. And if I might be so bold as to tempt the fates and say that it wouldn't *dare* be anything else. Of course,' she grinned impishly, her gaze settling on the soft curve of his smiling lips, 'last night wasn't too bad either. Although . . .' she let her forehead wrinkle into a worried frown, 'you do look a little tired to me this morning, Sadler.'

'I wonder why?' His dark eyebrows arched in mock surprise. Then he yawned sleepily, stretched and rolled on to his back, his gaze fixed somewhere up over their heads. 'I don't know why they call it "sleeping together",' he yawned again. 'I didn't get a wink of sleep last night.'

'Oh, liar!' Her hand was resting on his chest, so it was a simple matter for her to combine her accusation with the not-so-gentle tug of a few dark hairs.

'Ouch!' He quickly grabbed her wrists and pinned her back down on the bed. 'That hurt! What was that for?'

'Lots of reasons,' she answered boldly, even though she was having trouble breathing from the sheer weight of his body across her chest. 'For one thing, I feel *mean* this morning,' she bared her teeth at him and growled. 'And for another . . .' she paused, hesitating only a second, 'that was for letting me divorce you.'

'*Letting* you divorce me?' Eyes wide, Sadler released his grip as he sat up quickly to look at her. 'You sound like I had a choice, Cat. How was I supposed to stop you—lock you in the attic?' His expression narrowed slightly. 'You weren't the only one with a little pride, you know. I couldn't stop you, and I certainly wasn't going to force myself on a woman who didn't want me.'

'But don't you see, Sadler,' Catherine propped herself up on her elbow so she faced him, one hand still clutching the sheet in front of her in an unconscious display of modesty. Her nightgown, or what was left of it, was on the floor at the foot of the bed. 'If you'd tried to stop me, it probably wouldn't have reached the courts. I was divorcing you because I thought you didn't care any more. If only you'd fought the divorce, maybe . . .'

'No, Cat.' Sadler slowly shook his head, 'I don't think so. When I heard from your lawyer stating that you wanted nothing from me, not even my name, I took the hint.'

For the first time since the divorce she was realising how her actions must have affected him at the time, and his hurt then became her hurt now. 'Oh, Sadler,' her eyes filled with tears, 'I made an awful mess of everything, didn't I?'

'Sort of,' he agreed with a tender smile. Then he saw her expression and cradled her gently against his chest. 'But I think to be fair we'd have to share the blame. Your expectations were too great for me, or anyone else, to live up to. And for myself,' he paused reflectively, 'maybe I didn't expect enough from you. People have a way of living down to expectations too, and maybe that's what happened to you . . . to us.'

'But I wanted to be your wife, Sadler,' she shook her head, not in a gesture of denial but in a gesture of absolute futility. 'I wanted that more than anything else, Sadler. I tried, I really did.'

'I know you did, Cat,' he smiled softly at her tears. 'And I thought I was making it easy for you, but I can see now that what I did was all wrong.'

'Sadler?' Her voice was a soft breeze across his bare chest.

'What?' His lips rested lightly on her forehead.

'Why didn't you try and see me in all that time?' She picked up her chin and looked at him. 'Not once, in four years. Why?'

'Why didn't you try and see me?' He smiled when he saw her answering expression. 'Exactly! Both of us have spent the last few years trying to forget one another.' His eyes warmed. 'I guess it didn't work.'

'No.' Her expression reflected the glow she felt inside from his admission. 'It didn't work at all.' Happy that they were together at last, she settled down on his chest, his warm body and steady heart beat a constant reassurance to her contentment. 'Sadler?' she murmured softly. 'Can I ask you something?'

'Hmm.'

'If you wanted to forget all about me . . .' the sound of her own words brought a frown to her forehead, 'then why did you come back now—was it because of Parker's?'

'I said I was *trying* to forget you,' his chest heaved in a heavy sigh, 'but somehow or other I always managed to find out what you were doing. And I've known for a long time that Parker's was in deep financial trouble. So when it . . .'

Catherine sat up slowly, her expression hardening slightly as she put a little distance between them. 'You've known that Parker's has been in trouble for a long time?'

'Yes,' he hesitated briefly, 'I knew.'

'And you just sat back and watched and waited until I fell flat on my face before you offered to do anything to help?' It wasn't really a question, it was more like an accusation, and the first hint of anger slipped into Catherine's voice. 'If you wanted to invest, why didn't you do it earlier when it would have meant something to me and not waited until it was almost too late?'

'If you'd thought there was any chance, no matter how remote, of your getting the money on your own,' Sadler's voice was very calm, his answer well considered, 'would you have accepted my money then?'

The flashfire anger in Catherine's eyes disappeared behind a smile. 'No,' she shook her head, 'I wouldn't have taken your money if I thought for a second that I could raise it on my own.

'You know something, Sadler,' she continued, trying to look severe. 'It's unnerving for me to realise that you know me better than I know myself—even after all these years. It gives you an advantage that I'm not sure I like.'

'Oh, Cat!' Sadler tossed his head back and laughed, the sound of his laughter filtering happily around her. 'You've still got the greatest advantage in the world!'

'I do?' Catherine suddenly looked quite pleased with herself and wasn't sure why. 'What is it?'

'But if I told you that,' he grinned broadly, 'it would be checkmate, and then what would we do?'

'The queen would win?' she suggested softly, a light smile settling on her lips.

'She just might,' he acknowledged slowly, a strange expression crossing his face. 'Cat, I want to . . .'

A sudden chill ran down her spine and gesturing weakly she covered his lips with her fingertips. 'No,' she forced a bright smile, 'this is all getting too profound for early morning chatter. Let's get away from the metaphysical and back to something more physical.'

'OK.' Sadler was quick to agree, almost too quick. There was more to his reaction than the obvious pleasure of physical desire, because hidden among and behind the soft grey of his eyes was the unmistakable look of relief. 'I'm all for the physical.'

He reached for her, but she saw his coming and giggling, slipped out of his reach, pointing overhead as she did. 'Look!'

His puzzled gaze followed her pointing finger. 'The ceiling? What about it?' He looked at her worriedly.

'No, not the ceiling,' she laughed. 'The roof, or the skylight, to be exact. It's raining out—see!' She paused while he looked and listened to the gently falling rain, but he still didn't see any connection. 'We were going to the pond today,' she reminded him. 'But that sounds like an all-day rain to me. What *are* we going to do today, more checkers?'

Sadler's response to that was an immediate lowering of his dark lashes and a quick, highly exaggerated leer. 'We'll think of something to keep us busy,' his hand came slowly snaking its way under the covers for her.

'Besides *that*!' Catherine squealed as his hand landed squarely on her bare stomach. 'I thought you were tired?'

'Maybe I'm tired, kitten,' he agreed with a lazy grin. 'But I'm not dead, not yet.' He began to draw her slowly towards him.

'You know what I want . . . right now?' she asked, looking up at him.

'I think so,' he grinned.

'No,' she laughed, and shook her head. 'Not *that*—coffee—I want a cup of coffee.'

His lips froze in mid-pucker. 'Now?' He looked dismayed.

'Yes, coffee in bed, please.' She sat up, plumped up the pillow behind her shoulders, tucked the sheet up under her arms, folded the blanket top down across her lap, smoothed it off neatly like a little table, and looked up at him expectantly. 'With toast and jelly,' she added soberly, then quickly changed her mind. 'No, not the jelly, the jam—the strawberry jam, great gobs of it.'

With a defeated groan he rolled from his side of the bed and began to pull on his pants. 'Anything else?' he asked dryly over his shoulder. He was being facetious, of course, but it backfired.

'Yes!' Catherine quickly accepted his offer, her green eyes sparkling. 'As long as you've mentioned it there is something else. I want scrambled eggs, with just a touch of cheese, and a glass of orange juice—a tall one.'

'I'm sorry I asked.' He grinned goodnaturedly over his shoulder as he started to disappear, a step at a time, down the spiral staircase.

'I can't help it, Sadler,' she shook her head guilelessly. 'I'm starving! I haven't felt this hungry since . . .' she paused, 'I can't remember when. You wouldn't want to take carnal advantage of a starving woman, would you?' His reply to that was a snort, and she laughed when she heard it, the smile on her face staying long after she heard him in the kitchen. 'We don't have any fruit, do we?' She had to shout to make herself heard.

'No,' he called back from the kitchen doorway. 'And I'm beginning to think I made a mistake. It would be cheaper for me to clothe you than to feed you.'

'I should say so!' she laughed, peeping down under the sheet. 'Especially since I haven't a stitch on. And that reminds me, animal . . . you owe me a nightgown.' Suddenly chilly, she shivered and pulled up the blanket. 'Hurry up!' she called. 'I'm starting to get cold!'

She closed her eyes and snuggled back under the covers to wait for Sadler's return, his unnecessarily loud grumbling in the kitchen bringing an easy smile to her lips. Being up here with him these past few days had filled her with a contentment she hadn't felt in a very long time. And after last night, she sighed, she was going to be very careful not to do anything to ruin it.

'Hey!' Sadler's voice right next to the bed brought her out of her daydream in a hurry. 'What did you do, go back to sleep? I thought you said you were hungry?'

Catherine's eyes slowly widened with amusement as she took a long careful look at him. Barefooted and still naked to the waist, he had tucked a small dish towel down into the waistband of his pants and in his hands he carried a tray loaded down with everything she had asked for.

'Thank you, Sadler.' She demurely lowered her lashes

and turned her face slightly, trying valiantly not to smile as she watched him slide the tray across her lap. But the temptation was too great and her self-control too slight. 'Do you know,' she said slowly, peering at him from the corner of her eye, 'that one day you're going to make somebody a mighty fine little wife.'

The resulting look he gave her broke her up and she started to giggle. 'I'm sorry, Sadler,' she pinched her lips together in an effort not to laugh out loud, 'it's just that you look so . . . so . . .'

'Don't say it!' he warned, one eyebrow raised sharply in a fierce expression. 'Eat your breakfast,' he ordered mildly, sitting down next to her on the bed, 'before it gets cold.'

She stared at the amount of food on the tray. It looked enormous to her. Had she ordered all that? 'Is this all mine?'

'All of it, but this,' he agreed, reaching for the second cup of coffee on the tray. 'And eat all of it,' he ordered, frowning as he looked at her and her unfamiliar thinness. 'If you were trying to starve yourself to death, you were doing a darn good job. You can stand to gain a few pounds.'

'If I eat all this,' she told him slowly, 'I'll gain more than just a *few* pounds.'

'So?'

'So . . . will you love me if I do?' Her joking expression faded as the implication of her words began to register. It was supposed to be a joke, but suddenly it wasn't. Sadler hadn't told her that he still loved her, not once. In fact, her frown deepened, he had gone out of his way *not* to say it—*not* to make a verbal commitment. She put her fork down and stared at him. 'Well? Will you?'

'You don't really need to ask me that question, Cat,' his smile was her answer. 'I've never stopped loving you, kitten. I doubt if I ever could.'

Happy enough to explode, she lowered her lashes and

attacked her breakfast with renewed vigour. The food on her plate was perfect, the coffee was perfect, everything was perfect. In fact she had never been happier in her life than she was at that moment. It was only she was finishing the last of her breakfast that she began to learn one irrefutable fact of nature; there is no such a thing as 'perfect', and once the flaws are exposed to the light its disintegration may be slow, but it is inevitable.

'Is that a car I hear?' She put down her coffee cup and listened. 'Oh, it is, damn it,' she scowled. 'And I'll bet it's somebody from the garage. I forgot all about the car. I suppose they've located that stupid part and now they've sent someone out here to take the car back and fix it.'

'I doubt it, Catherine.' Sadler's use of her full name was as sobering as the look on his face as he slowly got to his feet and reached for his shirt. 'I'll see who it is. You stay here.'

'I'm not about to go with you,' she grinned. 'At least not while I'm dressed in nothing but a sheet!' Her teasing remark didn't draw the smile it should have, and as he pulled on his shirt and started down the stairs, she had an anxious little feeling that perhaps something might be wrong. She was certain there was something wrong when she saw the look on Sadler's face when he returned.

'Was it somebody from the garage?' she asked, fighting down the growing feeling of anxiety. 'Are they going to take the car back and fix it?'

'No, Cat.' He remained aloof, standing next to her bed and toying with a strange piece of paper in his hand. 'It wasn't anyone about the car.'

'Then who was it?' Her worried glance went to the piece of paper in his hand. 'What did they want?'

'Cat . . .' he said her name slowly, almost reluctantly, and in a tone of voice she had never heard before. Instinctively she braced herself. 'I don't know how you're going to take this, but I hope you're not going to get all upset. And you shouldn't if you'll just let me explain.'

With an introduction like that Catherine could do only one thing; she began to get upset. 'I don't understand,' her eyes widened, her puzzled gaze going repeatedly to the paper in his hand. 'Explain about what?'

'This.' He held up the paper. 'It's a message from the office.'

'From Maggie?' Catherine looked surprised. 'Has something happened at Parker's? Has . . .'

'No, Cat,' he shook his head quickly, 'it's not from Maggie. It's from McQuade Electronics.'

'Oh?' Both Catherine's voice and her body stiffened at precisely the same time. This was all beginning to sound familiar to her. 'How did McQuade Electronics know where to find you, Sadler? Or did they get in touch with Maggie and she told them?'

'Maggie didn't have to tell them,' he replied, his voice sounding strained. 'She didn't have to. I called them at the same time I called her from the store down the road. I had to leave a number where I could be reached.'

'But of course you did,' she agreed, her voice rising with the first hint of sarcastic displeasure. No wonder this all sounded familiar to her; she'd been through it a dozen times before. 'And at the same time you did that you had to make arrangements with somebody at the store to come out here and deliver any messages you might receive, right?' She thinned her lips as she watched his silent nod of agreement. 'And now,' she continued tightly, 'I suppose you're going to tell me there's some sort of an emergency that requires your immediate presence and you have to go running back.' A sudden thought brought a bitter smile to her lips. 'It's too bad your car isn't working, Sadler.' She paused, savouring the moment and all its implications. 'What *will* you do now?'

But her delicious moment was short lived. 'There's

nothing wrong with the car, Cat.' Sadler spoke the words, then waited.

'What do you mean, there's nothing wrong with the car?' Her eyes snapped. 'Did you fix it already? But you told me it was the starter or something like that. You said you couldn't repair it. You told me the garage had to do it and that it might take days. You said . . .' She finally stopped talking, her eyes narrowing with unwelcome understanding. 'There never was anything wrong with the car right from the beginning, was there, Sadler?'

He drew a tight breath. 'No.'

'And you could have left here any time you wanted to?' Catherine's question had varying tones—part anger, part uncertainty, part disbelief. 'And this entire weekend,' she continued after he nodded, 'this whole trip up here to the mountains was planned right from the beginning? It didn't just happen that way— you actually planned on staying here with me?'

'That's right,' he nodded.

His unflinching grey gaze held not a speck of remorse and perhaps Catherine's vivid imagination put more into his expression then was actually there, but all of a sudden everything fell into place for her—the huge amount of food, certainly way too much for only one person to eat, even over two weeks' time. And, her frown deepened, Sadler's great stroke of good luck by finding a closet full of clothes that just happened to fit him perfectly. And finding them in a closet that she knew now really had been empty. 'Those clothes aren't Bill's,' her voice was a cold chill in the warm cabin air, 'they're yours, aren't they?'

There was no need for him to pretend any longer, so he didn't. 'Yes, they're mine. I hung them in the closet before you woke up that morning. The rest of my stuff is still in the car. I thought that might be too much of a coincidence.'

'But why?' It was a plea as well as a question. 'Why

would you go to all that trouble—the car, the clothes?' she gestured. 'All that just to stay here for a few days. It doesn't make any sense, Sadler,' she frowned. 'And what's that got to do with your message from McQuade Electronics?'

'I'll explain everything,' he nodded, 'but you've got to understand that this message from McQuade Electronics turning up now is just a coincidence. I had intended to stay a week, or as long as you needed me.'

It sounded good, and her eyes momentarily softened. 'Why would you do that, Sadler?'

'I'd do anything for you, Cat,' his expression tightened. 'Don't you know that? When Smitty called me and I saw for myself what you were doing, I knew I had to do something. Getting you away was the first step, getting us back together was the second. And believe me,' he frowned lightly, 'that was the hardest part. I was afraid you'd seen through that story about the car breaking down and my having to go find someone to fix it.'

'But you did walk all the way back to the store?' Catherine wasn't sure. 'You must have,' she paused thoughtfully, 'otherwise they wouldn't have known where to find you just now.'

'I did walk to the store,' he acknowledged. 'I had to leave a number with my office where I could be reached in case of an em . . .'

'Emergency,' Catherine's voice prickled just a little. 'Some things never change, do they Sadler?'

'I've never stopped loving you, Cat,' he paused, '. . . if that's what you mean.'

It wasn't, but it was the right thing for him to say. 'And now we have to go back?' she asked wistfully, wishing she could have had just a few more days with him at the cabin.

'You don't have to go, Cat,' he shook his head. 'In fact the more I think about it, the better it might be if you didn't. I can take care of this business in a day or two and be back up here for the weekend.'

'No, Sadler,' she sighed. 'The bed'll be too cold now. I'll go back with you. I'd already decided to do that anyway.'

'Catherine . . .' He paused, pushing his fingers jerkily through the front of his hair. 'There's something else I have to say. I . . .'

'I know,' she shrugged sadly. 'You're sorry. So am I, Sadler, but there's nothing we can do about it.' Tossing the sheet to one side, she slid out of bed. 'I suppose I'd better get dressed if we're leaving. Do you want to start packing up the food while I do?'

'I'll get the stuff from the refrigerator,' he told her. 'But never mind the rest, I'll get that later. I'm in a hurry.'

'Suit yourself.' She started for the closet and her clothes. But then you always did, she added silently.

'Will I see you later?' Catherine stared at Sadler's sober profile as he pulled the Jag up to the kerb in front of her apartment.

'Of course you will, Cat.' He turned and smiled at her. 'You don't think I went through all that up at the cabin just to walk out of your life, do you?'

'No, I suppose not.' She smiled slowly to herself as she recalled exactly what Sadler had done at the cabin. But when she thought of this morning and the reason for their quick trip back, she frowned. 'Sadler,' she paused, 'I . . .'

But he wasn't paying any attention to her, his gaze fixed in a curiously blank stare out the window. It was an expression he had had on his face for the entire ride back, and whatever it was he was thinking had preoccupied his mind almost to the total exclusion of Catherine.

'Sadler?' she touched his arm. 'Are you all right? You've barely said two words to me the entire ride back.'

'It's not you, Cat,' he picked up her hand and kissed it, 'it's me. I'm sorry—I've got things on my mind.' He turned in the seat and faced her, his grip on her hand tightening until it was physically uncomfortable. 'Cat . . .' he frowned, not realising just how tight a grip he had, 'will you wait for me here at the apartment? I don't know how long this business thing is going to take me, but as soon as it's over I want to talk to you.'

'All right,' she agreed, her calm exterior no indication of her runaway heart. Of course he wanted to talk to her, he wanted them to get back together again. After the cabin, she smiled, what else could it be? 'I'll wait for you, Sadler.'

'Good.' He sighed deeply as if a great burden had just been lifted from his shoulders. 'Why don't you run on up?' he suggested. 'I'll get your suitcase and be right in.'

Sliding from the Jag, Catherine hurried into the building, the smile she felt inside bursting out all over her face. Wait until Smitty heard this! Wouldn't he be surprised? Bubbling over with the excitement of her news, she unlocked the front door, reaching down to pick up the afternoon paper before she stepped inside her apartment.

'Smitty?' she called, then stopped and listened. 'Smitty, I'm home, and guess what?' With a fleeting glance at the newspaper she tossed it on to the coffee table in the living-room, frowning to herself when it slid across the top and on to the floor. 'Smitty?' She picked up the paper and stared—there on the front page was the name Sadler McQuade. Curious, she immediately began to read; 'McQuade Electronics Acquires Stanton Chemical. Sources close to McQuade Electronics have revealed today that the takeover of Stanton Chemical had been in the works for months. It was only after the aquisition of a considerable block of Stanton stock that Sadler McQuade—the power and the brains behind McQuade Electronics—was able to force the merger.

Owning as he does now controlling interest in Stanton Chemical it was no . . .'

Catherine stopped reading and just stared at the article, the name *Stanton Chemical* leaping out at her from the type. Stanton Chemical—was it the *same* Stanton Chemical that Parker Plastics owned stock in—a considerable block of stock? Wasn't that an amazing coincidence? Her lips began to thin. Or was it?

'I can't stay, Cat,' Sadler's voice drifted by her as he headed down the hallway towards her bedroom. 'I'll put your suitcase in here and then I've got to go. I'll call you just as soon as I can.' Back at the living-room doorway he stopped, finally taking his first good look at her. 'What's the matter with you?'

'I'm not sure . . .' Catherine's stomach fluttered uneasily, her fingers curling tightly around the newspaper in her hand. 'Would you read this article for me?' She held out the paper.

'I can't, Cat,' he shrugged and shook his head. 'I haven't got time to . . .'

'*Read it!*' And before he had time to duck she threw it at him, hitting him squarely in the chest with it.

He swore lightly under his breath as he reached down for the newspaper, the look on his face when he stood up telling her he already had a good idea of what was in the paper without his having to read it.

'Will you let me explain, Cat?' Dark brows drew together sharply, his ruggedly handsome features compressed into granite-hard lines.

'I can hardly wait, Sadler.' Her face pale, Catherine thinned her lips and waited. 'Go ahead!' she demanded at last. 'Explain!'

'Cat, I . . .' He stopped and ran his fingers through his hair. 'Damn it, but I hate doing it like this.' He stared accusingly at the newspaper. 'The timing couldn't be worse.'

'Never mind the timing, Sadler,' she instructed, an

odd sense of detachment coming over her as she watched his fingers curl angrily around the newspaper. 'Just get on with it—explain. Tell me why I have this funny feeling in my stomach when I think of Stanton Chemical. Was that just an incredible stroke of good luck that Parker's owned stock in Stanton? Or was there something more to it than that? Tell me!'

He sighed and drew himself up to his full six foot four inch height. 'All right, Cat, here it is. But I want you to hear me out before you get crazy on me.' He paused, but all she did was stare at him. 'I didn't just happen to fall into that Stanton stock. I knew Parker's owned it, just like I knew that Parker's was in financial trouble. I made it a point to know.'

'Why—because of Stanton Chemical?' she stared at him. 'Was that your only interest in Parker's?'

'No.' Sadler's features compressed. 'I would have bailed Parker's out regardless of the Stanton stock.'

'Really?' she smiled thinly. 'Why do I find that so hard to believe?'

'I don't know. It's the truth.' He paused and waited, Catherine's expression remaining blatantly sceptical. 'You don't believe me?'

'No,' she shook her head, her pale eyebrows arching dramatically, 'not one word. But go ahead, I love a good lie.'

'It's not a lie, Cat!' His voice rose angrily. 'I know what this looks like, and I'm sorry. I've been wanting to tell you about this from the beginning. I even tried to,' he paused, 'several times up at the cabin, but something always happened and . . . well, the timing wasn't right.'

'And *this* is the right timing?' Her eyes widened with disbelief.

'No, of course not.' His hands curled into fists at his sides. 'I was planning on telling you all about this tonight. I didn't want you to find out like this, Cat. I knew the conclusion you'd jump to, and it's wrong.'

'Oh, but I don't think it is.' Catherine's voice was flat

and unemotional, her green eyes dull and lifeless. 'I think I've finally got it all straight in my mind.'

For a moment she stood there quietly digesting everything she had learned in the past few moments—all of it boiling down to only one thing; she had been used—badly. 'What I'm not clear on, Sadler,' she continued curiously, 'is why the stock proved to be so valuable to you. It's low-priced stock—it isn't even worth much. I know, I tried to put it up as security for another loan. It's worth nowhere near what I needed.'

'Not to you,' he admitted slowly, 'and not on the open market. But it was to me. I'd approached Stanton several times with a merger offer, but they didn't go for it, and I didn't own enough stock in Stanton to force it. I could have gone public and bought what I needed, or . . .' he paused and looked straight at her, 'I could get control of Parker Plastics and its assets.'

'Which you did.' Her lips didn't move as she spoke.

'Which I did,' he nodded. 'With enough stock I was able to force the merger and without going public to buy it at inflated prices.' He waited for some sign of understanding from her, but there was none. 'That's why I had to get back here today, Cat,' he continued, his voice sounding very far away. 'They've called an emergency stockholders' meeting to discuss it—although,' he allowed himself a very small smile of victory, 'now that I have the controlling interest there really isn't anything to discuss.'

'I always had a nagging feeling in the back of my mind,' Catherine sighed, 'That something wasn't right about the deal. It didn't make any sense to me, Sadler,' she mused quietly, her expression hardening. 'Why would you buy Parker's—generosity? No. Greed,' she thinned her lips. 'How much will that stock, *my* stock, bring you?'

'It doesn't matter, Cat,' he shook his head. 'That's not important.'

'Of course it's important—that's what this whole thing

is about!' She narrowed a smile at him. 'Humour me, Sadler—give me some figures to work with. You've told me this much, why not finish it? Let's see . . .' she paused and tapped her fingers together thoughtfully in front of her chest. 'In effect you paid sixty-three thousand dollars for some practically worthless stock—and that's not even taking into account what you acquired besides that—Parker Plastics, the inventory, the building,' she dismissed it all with an angry wave of her hand. 'We won't even consider that. Just talk to me about the stock. How much is it worth?'

'I told you,' he avoided answering her directly, 'it's a low-priced stock and on the open market it wouldn't be worth much. When the merger goes through it will increase in value, if it hasn't already, but . . .'

'Never mind all that!' she shouted, then struggled to bring her voice under control. 'I'm not talking about the market value—then or now. What I want to know, Sadler,' her voice lowered to an angry hiss, 'is what is this deal going to be worth to you?'

'All right, Cat, if you insist.' His expression hardened. 'Ultimately as much as ten times that amount. Perhaps more in the future.'

She whistled softly to herself as she put her head back against the sofa. 'That's not bad, Sadler,' she looked impressed. 'You invest a paltry sixty-three thousand for a projected return of a half to three quarters of a million dollars. That's not bad at all.' Her fury unleashed itself in a violent burst of temper and she flung herself at him. 'You rotten, sneaky, no good son of . . .'

'Stop right there, Cat!' He cut her off with an angry gesture of his own, his hands grabbing her flailing wrists. 'I knew you'd do this, I knew you'd take everything out of context. I didn't merely invest a "paltry" sixty-three thousand in the deal. I've invested a great deal of time and energy and money, and that's not even including the Parker Plastics deal. That stock was no good to you,' his grey eyes snapped back. 'But it was to me. And as far as any return is concerned, it's way down the road in the future and highly speculative at that. Anything can still happen.'

'Ah, but I'm not worried, Sadler,' Catherine sneered openly at him. 'Not with you in charge. You wouldn't *allow* the deal to sour—you've got the Midas touch.'

'You'd better hope that I do, Cat,' he countered harshly, finally releasing her wrists, 'because if you'd read the fine print in our contract you'll see where you stand to profit on this deal too. Once you get rid of your emotionalism you'll see that this is simply a business transaction, and one that stands to profit us both.'

'But one of us profits a little more than the other one, eh, Sadler?' Catherine tossed her head back and laughed bitterly, her red hair a swirling contrast to her pale face. 'The whole time I was worried about money I was sitting on a fortune and didn't know it. I could have held out for a lot more than the sixty-three thousand, couldn't I, Sadler?' He didn't immediately reply. 'Couldn't I!'

'*If* you had known about the merger,' he replied tightly, 'Yes, perhaps you could have.'

'And I should have checked.' Her voice grew very soft and self-condemning as she slowly walked back into the living-room. 'I had three days . . . I would have been able to discover something if only I'd checked into it instead of wasting my time fuming about you. No wonder you waited until the very last minute!' her voice hardened. 'I wasn't *supposed* to know anything about the merger!'

'I told you, Cat,' his lips thinned, 'I wanted to tell you up at the cabin, but I didn't want to take the chance of spoiling what we had. For the first time since the divorce, I . . .'

'Save it, Sadler!' she snapped. 'You weren't worried about spoiling what we had, any more than you were worried about my mental health. You were just afraid I'd find out about the merger and do something to spoil it.'

'That's not true!' His expression bordered on pure fury. He started towards her, then stopped. 'The merger deal had nothing to do with my wanting to be with you, Cat. I was worried about you.'

'Of course you were worried about me,' she smiled bitterly, putting her own interpretation on his explanation. 'I just said that. In fact you were so worried about my mental health that the first thing you did was try to gaslight me—putting clothes in empty closets and then telling me they were there the whole time!'

'Oh, Cat,' he looked at her disgustedly, 'you know why I did that.'

'I know a lot more than that, Sadler,' she put her hands on her hips. 'I know that that trip to the mountains wasn't because you were worried about my mental health. You were just worried that I'd find out and do something silly, like going to the Justice Department, or the Federal Trade Commission and maybe giving management at Stanton the chance to have you slapped with a preliminary injunction barring you from following up on your offer. So you just decided to play it safe and take me out of the picture entirely.

'Let's take poor old stupid Catherine away to the mountains for a while where she can't do any damage,' she gestured angrily with both hands. 'We'll keep her up there in the dark, like a mushroom, and feed her rubbish until the deal is finalised and she can't stir up any nasty trouble. And if you're *really* lucky,' she drawled sarcastically, her eyes filled with loathing, 'maybe you can wind it all up with a hop in the sack and a stroll down memory lane!'

Her hot temper exploded and she reached out for the nearest object to throw at Sadler. It was only a sofa pillow, but her aim was good and she had the momentary satisfaction of making him duck. 'You did it to me again, didn't you, Sadler?' She shook her head ruefully. 'I guess I'll never learn when it comes to you. You were right about one thing,' she thinned her lips, 'I should be committed—committed to the nearest institution for the incurably *stupid*. I can't believe you'd do this to me . . . I can't believe I let you!'

'You're not stupid, Cat,' Sadler said slowly, holding his own voice and temper in check. 'I never for one moment thought that you were. And I didn't *do* anything to you. As soon as you stop and think about this you'll see for yourself that what happened this weekend had nothing to do with the merger. It was a coincidence—an incredibly rotten piece of timing, but nonetheless a coincidence. Our going away together to the cabin had nothing—I swear it, Cat—absolutely *nothing* to do with the stocks or the merger.'

'Don't bother to swear to anything, Sadler,' Catherine's voice was very soft and unnaturally hollow-sounding, as if all the life had gone out of it . . . and her. 'Because I don't believe you. In fact,' she paused, 'I'll never believe you again—about anything.'

Her eyes began to fill with tears of disillusionment. 'I'll never forgive you for this, Sadler.' The look behind the tears was as hard and cold as frozen granite. 'The business deal was one thing, but why,' she choked on a sob, '*why* did you make me love you all over again? You even had me thinking it was my fault our marriage broke up and that maybe . . . maybe there was a chance we could . . .' she stopped talking and swallowed hard. 'You didn't have to make love to me, Sadler,' she paused again. It was getting harder and harder to talk and not cry. 'You already had everything from me that you wanted,' her voice broke again. 'You didn't have to do that to me too.'

'Catherine, don't do this.' His voice pleaded with her as he reached out for her, but she saw him through her tears and spun out of his reach, his hands falling helplessly back to his sides.

'Don't touch me, Sadler.' She spoke each word slowly and distinctly, the coldness in her eyes conveyed in each frozen syllable. 'Don't *ever* touch me again!'

CHAPTER NINE

'CATHERINE, stop it!' Sadler's jaw was a mass of tensing muscles. 'You're not even trying to understand me.' He grabbed her, spinning her around to face him. 'This isn't any good, Cat. It's not right—it's not fair!'

'Fair?' Catherine's expression flashed with new anger. 'You're a good one to talk about *fair*, Sadler—after what you did to me?'

'I didn't *do* anything to you, Cat. I keep telling you that!' He drew a tight breath. 'If I'm guilty of anything it's not finding a better way to handle all this. Maybe there was another way, but I'm damned if I know what it was. I can't, and I won't, have you believing I'd do something like that to you or anyone else. I would have told you all about it right from the beginning,' his voice softened, 'but I know your pride and your temper and I just couldn't take the chance . . . don't you see?'

She stood there staring icily at his fingers as they curled forcibly around her soft upper arm. 'Are you all through, Sadler?' she asked quietly. 'Because if you are . . .' She moved so quickly, so unexpectedly to break his grip that she easily succeeded in getting away from him. Angrily she pointed to the door. 'Get out!'

'No.' He shook his head firmly. 'I'm not leaving until I make you understand.'

'Then you can leave right away, Sadler,' she returned coolly, 'because I understand perfectly. I understand you were willing to do anything—go to any lengths to save your precious business deal, including making love to me. Well, congratulations, Sadler.' She swallowed a bitter sob. 'It worked perfectly.'

'As far as my making love to you goes, Cat,' Sadler's temper was beginning to get the better of him and his voice rose sharply, 'I don't see how that could have been part of my masterplan. If I remember the events of last night correctly,' he paused and thinned his lips, '*you* were the one who started it, and I don't recall your putting up much of a fight after that.'

'Oh . . . cheap shot, Sadler!' Catherine's cheeks flared. 'But then from you I should expect it.'

He closed his eyes and ran his hand tiredly across his troubled brow. 'All this isn't getting us anywhere,' he sighed deeply. 'We're beginning to say things we don't mean.'

'Speak for yourself, Sadler!' She began to walk towards the front door. 'I've meant every single word I've said. But what makes all this worse,' she swallowed suddenly, 'is that I believed you—I believed *in* you. And last night I even let myself believe we had a second chance together. I thought you'd come back into my life because you wanted *me*—you couldn't live without *me*. But it wasn't *me* that you wanted.' She shook her head slowly, her eyes filling again with unwelcome tears. 'You wanted my stock!'

'I did want you last night,' Sadler's hands were fists at his sides. 'And in spite of this ridiculous fight, I still want you, Cat, I always have. You haven't been out of my thoughts since the divorce,' his voice softened, 'not once. Parker's and the merger were only an excuse to see you again. *You* were the reason. You . . .'

'Oh, stop it!' she shouted. 'Save your breath, Sadler, because I don't believe anything you're saying.' She opened the door and held it. 'Just get out!'

'Get out?' Smitty's voice sounded confused. 'I was just coming in.' His eyes narrowed slightly as he saw the furious expression on Catherine's face. 'I didn't expect you back so early, Catherine.' He paused. 'Something go wrong?'

'Wrong?' She started to laugh bitterly. 'That's probably the understatement of the year! Say goodbye to Sadler,' she suggested in flat tones, 'because he's in a big hurry, and if I have anything to say about it we'll never have to see him again.'

Smitty, his arms full of groceries, turned to Sadler and shrugged. 'I guess it didn't work out like you planned,' he shook his head sadly.

'Planned?' The word rekindled Catherine's fury and she turned slowly to glare at Sadler. 'It turned out exactly as he had it planned—didn't it, Sadler?'

'Catherine . . .' Sadler's grey eyes were the colour of thunder clouds. 'One of these days,' he paused, his face so close to hers his breath made her blink, 'I'm going to take you over my knee. I can see now that that was something I should have done a long, long time ago. You may have been your daddy's precocious little darling,' he continued tightly, 'but you're not that any more. And right now you're just a pain in the neck. A damn good spanking might do wonders for your disposition. It certainly couldn't hurt it!'

Catherine took a step backwards—not out of any fear of him, but to get a better glare at him. 'Try it, Sadler,' she dared him, her hands going to her hips, her green eyes flashing. 'I'd like to see you try it! You lay one hand on me and I'll have you slapped in jail so fast it'll make your head spin!'

She smiled nastily at him. 'What do you think the stockholders would think of you then, Sadler? Do you think they'd be happy in a merger with your company with you in jail on an assault and battery charge? And a *woman* at that!'

Her tirade produced little more than a quirk to Sadler's lips. 'If they knew who the woman was,' he countered smoothly in icy tones, 'they'd probably give me a standing ovation.' His grey eyes gleamed threateningly. 'It's almost worth it, Cat.' He took a small step in her direction.

'Ho-ly cow!' Smitty's exclamation was punctuated with a long, soft whistle, his eyes darting from one to the other. 'What's going on here?'

'I'll tell you, Smitty.' Catherine seemed eager to reply and perhaps switch the subject away from the threatened spanking. 'What do they call it when you suddenly see things clearly for the first time?' She pursed her lips thoughtfully. 'A revelation!' she snapped her fingers triumphantly. 'That's just what it was—a revelation. You might even say it was spiritual in concept.'

'Oh, shut up, Catherine!' Sadler started towards her, then stopped, changed his mind and stormed out of the apartment, slamming the door so hard behind him that both Smitty and Catherine flinched.

With the sound of the slamming door still an angry echo in the background, Smitty slowly shook his head. 'Catherine . . . Catherine . . . Catherine . . .' he sighed.

'Don't "Catherine-Catherine" me!' she snapped. 'It's not my fault.' She turned around and started for her bedroom, talking to Smitty over her shoulder as she did. '*I'm* not the one who bought Parker's under false pretences. *I'm* not the one who hid the fact that some stock Daddy owned in the company name wasn't as worthless as it appeared. And I'm certainly *not* the one who stands to make a small fortune because of that stock and some really clever business merger!'

Smitty came to a halt at her bedroom doorway, watching her systematically slam closet doors and bang dresser drawers, all under the pretence of putting her clothes away. 'I can usually follow you, Catherine,' he frowned, 'but not this time. What are you talking about?'

'I'm talking about Sadler.' She sat down on the foot of her bed, her hands clasped tightly in her lap. 'It's in today's newspaper,' she sighed, 'but briefly this is it.' She took a deep breath and waited for Smitty to return from the kitchen before she continued. 'Sadler wanted to acquire another company—Stanton Chemical—but they didn't want it. And I can't say that I blame them,' she added sourly. 'If I only knew then what I know now I . . .'

'Sadler?' Smitty reminded her patiently.

'Oh . . . well,' she paused, 'Sadler had some stock in the company, but not enough for a controlling interest. He could have made an offer for what stock he needed, but the stockholders would need a good deal more money than what it's currently valued. Ever clever, our dear Sadler remembered my father had stock in the very same company, but it was part of the assets. He couldn't have one without the other, so he . . .'

'Took over Parker Plastics,' Smitty finished her sentence with a knowing nod. 'And got the stock he needed for a controlling interest in Stanton.'

'Right you are—and it's all over now but the shouting.' Catherine's frown deepened. 'Now do you understand why I'm mad?'

Smitty's brow puckered. 'No, Catherine,' he slowly shook his head, 'I don't—not really.'

Stunned by his reply, Catherine could only stare in disbelief. 'What do you mean "no"? I just explained to you that Sadler bought into Parker's—*not* to bail me out like he pretended, but to feather his own damn nest!'

'OK,' nodded Smitty, 'so Sadler did all that. So what? The facts remain the same, Catherine. Parker Plastics was literally *hours* away from bankruptcy. That stock was no good to you—*you* certainly weren't going to merge with Stanton. Ask yourself one simple question,' his voice softened. 'Ask yourself how you'd be reacting right now if it had been a complete stranger who had bought Parker's and the stock, and not Sadler. Parker's has only one chance for survival, and a slim chance at that. So if Sadler makes a profit by the deal,' he shrugged, 'who's to say that's wrong?'

'But he didn't trust me enough to tell me about it!' Catherine's eyes widened with wounded pride. 'He purposely kept me in the dark by taking me up to that cabin in the mountains and . . .' she swallowed hard, her voice fading slightly, '. . . and keeping my mind on other things. You know the saying "All's fair in love and war?" Well, Sadler's brought it to an art.' She tried, but she couldn't stop the tears from forming. 'Love—war—it doesn't make any difference to him, it's all one and the same.'

'I'll admit that I didn't know anything about the merger,' admitted Smitty with a shake of his head, 'or for that matter what you're talking about now. But I do know that the merger wasn't the reason he took you to the mountains. Catherine . . .' he paused, his frown deepening, 'I don't think you realise how worried we were about you—Sadler, Maggie, *all* of us. When Sadler suggested the cabin and said a few days up there might do you some good, I . . .'

'Talk's cheap, Smitty,' Catherine's lips thinned. 'Sadler can *say* anything he wants to. He even told me that was why he brought me to the cabin, but it's what *happened* that really counts.'

'I don't believe that,' Smitty shook his head. 'The only thing he had on his mind was you—he still loves you, Catherine.'

'No, Smitty,' she sighed, and got to her feet. 'You're only saying that because you don't know what happened up at the cabin. You don't . . .' She stopped talking, a stranger expression slowly crossing her face. 'I think this is the last time I'm going to talk about Sadler McQuade. From now on, as far as I'm concerned, Sadler McQuade doesn't exist.' She walked to the edge of her bed, pulled back the covers and looked as if she was about to crawl in.

'You're not going to bed, are you?' Smitty's eyes mirrored his sudden concern. All he could think of was last week and Catherine's retreat to her bed. What if she was right back where she started?

'As a matter of fact, I am,' she smiled thinly, 'but don't look so worried, because I have absolutely no intention of taking to my bed again. I'm going to take a nap—and then a nice long soak in the tub. Then I'm going to wash my hair and go out.'

'Out? Out *where*?' demanded Smitty. Catherine's reply coming as a surprise to him. 'You just got home.' He thinned his lips, his protective instincts instantly aroused. 'When did you make plans to go out—and with whom?'

'Just now, actually.' Catherine sat on the edge of her bed and smiled, flipping her foot and watching her shoe sail halfway across the floor. 'And I don't know who the lucky man is yet.' She pursed her lips thoughtfully. 'Maybe I'll call Dick and see what he's doing.'

'Dick?' Smitty's chilly voice was tinged with disbelief. 'This is some change—you told me you couldn't stand him.'

'That was *then*,' Catherine rationalised with an indifferent shrug, 'and this is now. I'm sure Dick had qualities that I didn't see before. What can you learn from a couple of dates?' she asked innocently, but Smitty wasn't impressed. So she frowned and continued with her argument. 'He wasn't that bad . . . he deserves a second chance.'

'Oh?' Smitty smiled strangely at her. 'What are you doing, practising a little selective second-chance giving? What about Sadler? Instead of pretending that he doesn't exist I think you should wait a few days, until you've cooled off, and then sit back and look at everything objectively. Although,' he scowled to himself, 'I don't know if that's possible. You never have been objective when it comes to Sadler. Maybe that's what the problem is.'

'The problem is,' Catherine snapped, 'that "objective" and "Sadler" are two words that can't possibly be used in the same breath. When it comes to Sadler the key word is "subjective", not "objective". Sadler manages to subjugate everybody he meets. I haven't been free of him for four years,' she continued in a steely calm voice which did more to worry Smitty than if she had shouted, 'and I think it's about time that I was.' Her expression suddenly hardened. 'I thought I just said I didn't want to talk about him?'

'That's OK by me,' Smitty shrugged, diplomatically refraining from pointing out that she has been the one doing most of the talking. 'I'm not going to argue with you. You're a big girl now. I only hope you know what you're doing.'

'I know exactly what I'm doing,' Catherine declared tightly. 'I've wasted four years of my life over Sadler, but not any more. From now on I'm going to start enjoying myself!'

Catherine smiled at herself in the full-length bedroom mirror, then running her hands slowly down her hips she turned around, giving herself the benefit of all possible angles. Not bad, she admitted immodestly, glancing down over her shoulder at the pale lavender dress and the way it clung in all the right places. Lavender with red hair was outrageous, but Catherine felt outrageous. Dick should really like this dress.

For a moment the outrageous Catherine actually let herself believe that she really cared what Dick thought about anything, but it was too much of a pretence, and with a disgruntled sigh she collapsed on the edge of her bed.

How long has it been since that ill-fated weekend with Sadler up at the cabin? A month? Maybe more? Catherine ran her hand over her eyes—oh, she knew how long it had been. She knew *exactly*. Four weeks, three days, and . . . she actually started to glance at the clock next to her bed, then in a fit of disgust jumped to her feet.

Why wasn't this working? she demanded an answer from the girl in the lavender dress. To forget one man you simply involved yourself with another one. It was simple—there was nothing to it. Loving someone is a learned experience; she had learned to love Sadler, therefore it stood to reason that with a little time she could learn to unlove him.

Maybe it was Dick's fault. Unconsciously Catherine's skin crawled, and that was just from thinking about Dick. It was even worse when he actually touched her. But she couldn't really blame Dick, she'd been out with several men lately and they had all had the same effect on her.

She'd just have to keep trying, that was all, and determination flared behind the green eyes. She was *not* going to sit home alone—or worse yet, with Smitty and Maggie—and listen to her arteries harden while Sadler and Sophia were going out practically every night. They were as good as joined at the hip, she scowled sourly as she recalled the latest occasion when she had run into them. Sophia was all over Sadler like a bad case of the measles—all that pawing and heavy breathing, she sneered, it was a small wonder Sophia didn't hyperventilate herself.

Catherine's conscience stabbed her and she actually flinched from the self-inflicted pain. Her own behaviour that night had been nothing to brag about, and she had no one to blame but herself if Dick expected a little more that night than a hurried handshake at the door.

Maybe she should go away for a while—maybe she should look for a job—maybe she should . . . Out of maybes, Catherine threw herself down on her bed and stared up at the ceiling. The plain truth was—she didn't know what she wanted to do.

'Catherine?' Maggie's knock came softly on the bedroom door. 'May I come in?'

'Sure, Maggie,' Catherine sighed, and glanced at the door. 'Come on in.'

'I . . . er . . .' Maggie hesitated in the doorway, a peculiar look on her face, her hands held out of sight behind her back. 'I just stopped in for a minute.' Her eyes fell to the lavender dress that Catherine was wearing. 'Are you just coming in—going out—or did you sleep in that thing?'

'None of the above,' Catherine laughed, and sat up. 'I

was just trying it on—it's new. Do you like it?' She turned around. 'It's for a date I have tonight.'

'It's very nice,' nodded Maggie. 'Another date with Dick?'

'As a matter of fact, yes.' Catherine narrowed her eyes and waited for the lecture she was sure was going to come. She'd already heard it all from Smitty. 'Well? Aren't you going to say something?'

'Nope.' Maggie shook her head. 'It's none of my business. I just stopped by on the way to work this morning to show you something.' She pulled her hands out from behind her back and handed Catherine the magazine she had been keeping there. 'Here.'

Catherine automatically took it, her expression losing a lot of its colour when she saw the cover. It was Sadler, looking right at her—and her stomach flipped. She hadn't been prepared. 'Damn it, Maggie!' her green eyes flared, 'I don't want this!' And with that she tossed it into the wastepaper basket next to the dresser.

If Maggie was upset by Catherine's action she didn't show it. 'It's your copy,' she shrugged. 'You can do anything you want to with it. I just thought you'd like to have it. It's not on the stands yet, but it will be.'

Catherine closed her eyes and turned her back to Maggie, hoping to compose herself before she risked turning around again. That had been a stupid thing to do, throwing that magazine away. It made it look as if Sadler could still upset her, and everybody knew *that* wasn't true. 'Thank you, Maggie,' it was a smiling Catherine who now turned around to face her, 'I'll read it later.'

'In the wastepaper basket? Wouldn't it be easier if you took it out?' Maggie waited, but all Catherine did was smile. 'It's a good picture of him,' she continued. 'Of course Sadler's so darn good-looking it's impossible for him to take a bad picture. It's not every day either that you get your picture on a news magazine as prestigious as that one. Sadler . . .'

'Don't you have to be to work today?' Catherine's sullen look went pointedly to the clock next to her bed.

'I do,' Maggie took the hint and laughed. 'And I'm going—right now.' She turned around and waved. 'Talk to you later, Catherine. 'Bye!'

She was gone, and Catherine continued to stand there staring at the corner of the magazine peeping out from the top of the basket. She didn't care if Sadler got his picture on a magazine cover! She didn't care if he spent every night with Sophia! She didn't care that he hadn't called, not once, since their fight! She didn't care! Sighing loudly and condemning herself for an appalling lack of will-power, she slowly bent over and picked the magazine out of the wastepaper basket. She cared.

CHAPTER TEN

CATHERINE knew it was more than a little 'chat' that Smitty and Maggie had in mind when Smitty brought out the twenty-year-old Scotch. 'Must be serious,' she glanced from Smitty to Maggie and back. 'What's up?'

Maggie looked uncomfortable as she exchanged what was supposed to be a furtive glance with Smitty, her fingers nervously smoothing imaginary wrinkles from the lap of her dress as she did.

'This is starting to look like a gathering for the reading of a will,' joked Catherine, and lowered her voice. 'I have gathered you all here today . . .' the smile on her lips slowly faded; they were just staring at her and it was beginning to make her nervous. 'Something's the matter—what is it?'

Unable to hold it back any longer, Maggie suddenly beamed, at almost precisely the same time Smitty smiled at Catherine with the silliest grin she'd ever seen. Standing behind Maggie's chair, he put his hands on her shoulders and grinned even wider. 'We're going to get married,' he announced.

Nothing could have pleased Catherine more than that did, and with a wild whoop of delight she threw her arms around both of them, stooping to kiss first Maggie on the check and then Smitty. 'Well, it's about time!' she scolded with a smile. 'I was starting to wonder if the two of you were ever going to come to your senses and realise you belong together.'

Her gaze landed on the bottle of Scotch and with a displeased gesture she waved it aside. 'This is call for a celebration, but not with Scotch. Haven't we got some champagne somewhere, Smitty?' Her happiness bubbling over, her delight flew back to the couple. 'I can't tell you how happy I am for both of you. You're my two favourite people in the whole world and you should be together. It's where you've always belonged.'

'I know for a fact that if Smitty had had his way,' Catherine continued with a half-hearted scolding, 'he would have married you long before now.' Her sober frown dissolved into a giggle of pure delight. 'Oh, I can't pretend to be mad,' she laughed. 'Not when I feel so good.'

'Try and hold on to that feeling, Catherine, when we tell you the rest of our news.' Smitty's voice was still happy, but now there was an unwelcome undercurrent of strain in it. Even the beaming Maggie's expression was beginning to look a little tight.

'Oh?' Catherine's smile slipped slightly. 'Don't tell me this is going to be one of those "good news"—"bad news" things?"

'No, not really,' Smitty shook his head, his fingers curling around Maggie's hand in a comforting gesture. 'But it's going to have a great deal to do with your point of view and how you're willing to accept it. Catherine . . .' he paused and looked down at Maggie. 'Maybe you'd better tell her.'

Maggie's sharply arching brown eyebrows told Smitty what she thought of that idea. 'I think you'd better tell her, dear,' she suggested sweetly.

'Well, somebody'd better tell me!' Catherine couldn't imagine what the problem was. 'Is somebody sick?'

'No, no,' Smitty quickly shook his head. 'Nobody's sick—I would have told you that. It's . . .' he paused, 'Sadler.'

'Sadler?' Catherine swallowed quickly, but the dry lump in her throat wouldn't go away. With Smitty and Maggie's announcement of marriage fresh in her mind, she put two and two together and came up with what she thought was the obvious conclusion. Sadler and Sophia had been seeing a considerable amount of one another lately; were they about to make it permanent? 'He's getting married,' she squeaked in a little voice.

'Who is?' Smitty looked confused.

'Sadler.' Catherine was confused.

'I don't know that!' Smitty glanced at Maggie. 'Why didn't you tell me Sadler was getting married?'

'Because I didn't know it,' Maggie shrugged, and looked at Catherine. 'Who told you?'

'Oh never mind,' Catherine groaned, and shook her head weakly. 'I thought that's what you were going to tell me. Go on,' she sighed. 'What about Sadler?'

Smitty drew a deep, deep breath before he replied. 'Sadler's decided Parker's can't be saved, Catherine. He's closing it down for good.'

Like a slow-motion movie with the voice out of sync, Catherine watched his lips silently from the words, the actual sound not registering until seconds later. When they did her face lost all its colour—even the freckles across the bridge of her nose faded. 'What did you say?' she whispered hoarsely. For a moment she had thought that hearing that Sadler was getting married was the worst possible news she could have heard. And maybe in the long run it would have been, but this . . . this was almost as bad.

'I said,' Smitty saw the look on her face and his voice softened emotionally, 'that Parker's is going out of business. I'm sorry, honey.'

Catherine's knees buckled and her legs started to give out, refusing to hold up her weight. If Smitty hadn't anticipated such a reaction from her and had been ready to react—in this case with a chair—she surely would have crumbled to the floor. 'But why . . .' she whispered, looking into first one face, then the other. 'Why?'

'Oh, Catherine,' Maggie looked as if she was on the verge of crying, 'do you really have to ask that question? You knew your father—times change, technology changes, but he didn't. Even with Sadler's money and connections behind him, Parker's would have been a losing proposition for ever. It wasn't an easy decision for

Sadler to make, you know,' Maggie shook her head lightly. 'I know that for a fact. I've watched him these past few weeks and I know how much it took for him to come to that conclusion, but it was the only conclusion he could make.'

'I see.' Catherine swallowed dryly, the sudden tightness in her chest making it hard for her to breath. 'Sadler got what he really wanted, the stock—and now there's no reason to keep Parker's going, so he's going to shut it down and put everybody out of work. It's almost funny when you think about it,' she laughed bitterly, 'because that was Sadler's great argument to me. "Catherine",' she imitated Sadler's low masculine voice, 'you've got to consider your employees. You can't sit back and let Parker's fold when I can save it! Let *me* take it over! Let *me* run it!'

'I knew you were going to say that,' Maggie's voice hardened slightly, 'or something just like it. But that's not true, and Sadler *did* consider the employees—all of them—before he made that decision. The pension fund that your father started, Sadler's guaranteed somehow, so that the few employees old enough to retire can still draw on it. The rest of the employees are either going to be absorbed in one of Sadler's other companies or, if they want to, they can choose to be retrained in another field. None of which, I might add,' Maggie looked directly at Catherine, 'would have happened if you'd been forced to close down Parker's yourself.'

'And Sadler marches on . . . and on . . . and on,' Catherine drawled bitterly. 'A little bit like Sherman burning his way to Atlanta.'

'You're wrong.' Maggie's troubled expression reflected her divided loyalties. 'Sadler's not destroying anything, Catherine. If anything, it's just the opposite. Parker's was unsalvageable when Sadler took it over. All he's done is make it as easy as he can for everyone concerned. I wouldn't call that destructive.'

'Maybe not,' Catherine reluctantly agreed. 'But I

can't help but marvel at the way everything works out in Sadler's favour. He bought up Parker Plastics for the stock we owned in another company, the company he was really interested in to begin with—saved himself a considerable piece of change in the process and managed to pull off the mini-grand merger of all time.' Catherine waved her hand irritably. 'And now with the demise of Parker Plastics he's got the additional benefit of a dandy little tax loss.' Her expression hardened. 'I'm surprised that in his spare time he hasn't discovered a cure for the common cold!'

'What *is* your problem when it comes to Sadler?' Smitty's voice frosted over. 'I didn't understand it four years ago and I don't understand it now! Instead of being relieved—I'm not even going to mention *grateful*—that nobody's going to be out in the streets, you're busy sniping Sadler in the back!'

Catherine drew a long deep breath, but it didn't help. Neither did the look on Smitty's and Maggie's faces. They were upset with her, even disappointed, but it was nothing compared to the way she felt about herself. How could she hope to explain her feelings about Sadler when she didn't understand them herself?

'I suppose you'll go on working for Sadler?' Catherine forced a smile as she looked at Maggie. 'You're the best secretary anybody could ever have. I'm sure he realises that too.'

Maggie allowed herself a small smile of pride, but contrary to the smile she shook her head no. 'He asked me to stay on and work for him,' she admitted. 'It was quite an offer. I'd be working as his private secretary, with lots of travel and a generous pay increase.'

'And you turned that down?' Catherine's eyes widened. 'Oh, Maggie,' she sighed, 'I hope you didn't let anything I've ever said about Sadler influence your decision not to stay with him. Just because I can't get along with him that doesn't mean that you . . .'

'No, no,' Maggie quickly shook her head, 'it wasn't

that—I just had a better offer, that's all.' Her smile warmed as she looked at Smitty. 'The money's not all that good, but the benefits couldn't be beaten. My decision not to stay with Sadler didn't have anything to do with you, Catherine. On second thoughts,' she frowned, 'maybe it did have something to do with you, but not in the way you think. Do you remember the other day when I brought over that magazine and you threw it in the wastepaper basket?' Catherine nodded and Maggie continued. 'It dawned on me than that I was doing the same thing you were. Smitty and I love one another, but I was putting up one obstacle after another—little things, things that didn't mean anything. Just like you're letting false pride and plain craziness keep you and Sadler apart. So I tracked Smitty down that very day and told him. It's just that simple, Catherine.'

'No, it's not, Maggie,' sighed Catherine, her voice nothing more than a whisper. 'It's not simple at all.' But she didn't want to talk about Sadler now, or even think about him, when she had something so happy to consider. 'What are your plans? What are you going to do after the two of you are married?'

Smitty answered with a big smile. 'With my service pension and what both of us have saved, we're going to travel a little and maybe buy a small house in the country with a garden and a . . .'

'He's right, you know.' Catherine's hand flew to cover her mouth. She hadn't intended to say that, it just popped out.

'Who is?' frowned Smitty, then his eyes widened as he realised Catherine was talking about Sadler. 'Surely you're not referring to Sadler? You can't be.' Smitty winked at Maggie. 'It must be the excitement of the occasion. I think Catherine's feverish. She must be,' he shook his head. 'She didn't actually say Sadler was right about something, did she?'

'We must have misunderstood her,' Maggie smiled

secretly. 'That doesn't sound like Catherine to me either.'

'All right, all right!' scowled Catherine lightly. 'There's no need for the two of you to carry on like that. All I said was Sadler was right about closing Parker's. I *didn't* say he was right about everything. Even Sadler makes mistakes.'

'Quite true.' Smitty smiled as he picked up his glass for a toast. 'Here's to mistakes—without them how would we know when we were right? And here's to us,' he looked tenderly at Maggie. 'And to Catherine and Sadler, too,' he grinned. 'Why not?'

'I don't think you can propose a toast to yourself,' Catherine laughed, conveniently ignoring the part about her and Sadler.

'That's silly. Who knows better than I do what I want from life?' Smitty held up his glass again. 'Here's to us.'

'But you . . .' Catherine broke off her protest and grinned. 'You're right, Smitty,' their glasses clincked. 'Here's to us.'

'Are you going to be all right?' Smitty's question to Catherine was compounded by a worried frown. 'You look funny to me.'

'Thanks,' she grinned impishly, 'but isn't that a strange question coming from you—under the circumstances? After all,' she brushed an affectionate kiss on his cheek, 'it's a wedding, and I always look *funny* at weddings. Especially this one. You've been a father to me, and Maggie . . .' she paused, 'I just don't know what I would have done without Maggie these past few years. I love you both and I'm losing you both at the same time. I think I have every right to look funny.'

'It's more than that, Catherine.' Smitty shook his head as he grabbed her arm and pulled her into an empty ante-room, Catherine's kiss doing nothing to remove the worried frown from his face. 'I watched your face this afternoon when you saw Sadler show up here at the courthouse with Sophia. But what could I do?' he continued with a helpless shrug. 'When Maggie told Sadler we were getting married, he insisted on giving us a wedding gift—and considering his gift is our entire honeymoon to Hawaii I could hardly ask him not to come to the wedding today. And he is a witness,' he frowned. 'I'm just sorry for you that he had to bring Sophia along.'

'Don't be,' Catherine patted his arm reassuringly. 'Sadler's got every right to go anywhere he wants to and with anyone he chooses. It has nothing to do with me, so don't worry.'

'I only wish it was that easy,' Smitty sighed, 'but it isn't. I *do* worry about you. Especially today when I know you're going to be on your own for the next few weeks. Maggie and I are leaving straight for the airport—just as soon as she gets done talking to Sadler.' He glanced affectionately through the open doorway at his brand new bride. 'And that,' he turned back to Catherine, 'means you're going to be *alone* in the apartment.'

'I've been *alone* before,' Catherine whispered the word exactly as Smitty had done. 'I promise to eat all my breakfast,' her eyes twinkled as she raised her right hand in a gesture of vowing. 'I'll brush my teeth after every meal. I'll get eight hours' sleep every night. I'll . . .'

'OK, OK,' frowned Smitty, 'I get the point. You're a big girl now, so you're able to take care of yourself.'

'Yes, I am, and you are *not* to worry about me! That's an order.' She put a stern look on her face. 'Have you remembered everything?'

'I think so,' Smitty tapped his breast pocket and nodded.

'Travellers cheques?' she continued. 'Hotel reservations? Plane tickets? I know your bags are all packed, they're in the car. So what are you waiting for?'

'For one thing, the other half of my honeymoon,' he glanced up, saw Maggie start towards them and smiled, slipping his arm through hers as soon as she came near enough. 'Now I've got everything,' he grinned.

'Give Catherine a kiss,' he ordered Maggie. 'And let's go. If we stay around the courthouse any longer we're going to miss our flight.'

'Ooh!' Maggie sighed, her eyelids fluttering with adoration as she looked lovingly at Smitty. 'The masterful kind—I love it! We haven't been married ten minutes and already he's taking charge!'

Maggie's radiant smile lost some of its glow as she looked closely at Catherine's strained expression. 'Are you going to be all right?'

'Yes! And will everybody stop asking me that. You're beginning to give me a complex.' Catherine pointed sternly towards the side door. 'Now go. If you wait any longer the judge will think you're having second thoughts about the marriage and he just might take his ceremony back.'

Amid hugs and kisses and badly disguised tears, Catherine smiled as she watched Maggie and Smitty hurry out of the courthouse doors. She was envious, just for a moment, but she was honest enough to admit it. Perhaps envy wasn't a sterling quality, but it was a human one, and as the large wooden door slowly closed behind Smitty and Maggie Catherine envied them the happiness they were going to share.

Weddings! Bah! A lone tear trickled down her cheek and she quickly wiped it away with her gloved hand. Why does everyone always cry at weddings? Catherine had an answer, at least for this wedding. It was because the last time the four of them had been together at a wedding, she was marrying Sadler and Maggie and Smitty had been the witnesses. An ironic twist of fate had put them in the exactly opposite positions today.

She was beginning to get maudlin, and shaking her head in an effort to push such thoughts away, she turned and hurried towards the side door. So far today she considered herself lucky—Sadler and Sophia had exchanged precious few words with her, and that was exactly the way Catherine wanted it. Aside from a brief nod and a crisp 'hello, nice day for the wedding' Catherine's conversation with Sadler was nil. He was entitled to go out with anyone he wanted to, including Sophia, but Catherine was under no obligation to hang around and become part of their entertainment.

'Catherine! Wait a minute!' Sophia's voice prevented her from taking that final step outside. 'I'd like to talk to you for a moment, if I may?'

Frowning, Catherine turned to face them, her green eyes already set in hard expectation of seeing Sadler again. Only Sadler wasn't there—Sophia was alone.

'Sadler's gone to get the car,' Sophia explained when she saw the inquisitive look on Catherine's face. 'And while he has,' she continued quickly, 'and we have this chance to talk, I think we should.'

'Really?' Catherine forced herself to be polite. 'I'm in a hurry, Sophia, and as far as that goes I don't see that we have anything to talk about.' She was *almost* polite.

'I think we do,' Sophia disagreed, thinning her bright red lips. 'Sadler—' she paused. 'I want to talk to you about Sadler.'

Catherine actually laughed. 'If you're having trouble handling Sadler,' her green eyes widened, 'there's not a thing I can tell you that will help. You're on your own, Sophia.'

'You've misunderstood me,' Sophia's voice hardened. 'I don't want *you* to tell *me* anything. You're right, there's nothing you can tell me about Sadler, but there is something I can tell you.'

'Oh?' Catherine got all pinched-faced. She didn't care for the tone of Sophia's voice, which wasn't all that surprising. Lately she didn't care a whole lot for Sophia. 'What?'

Sophia drew a deep breath before she replied. 'I'm in love with Sadler.'

The unexpected confession brought Catherine up

short, but only for a second. 'So what?' she shrugged indifferently. 'Don't tell me—tell him!'

'I already have,' Sophia's voice softened. 'Sadler knows it.'

'Well, that's just dandy,' Catherine returned sweetly, her voice heavy with sarcasm. 'But I really don't want to hear all this. It doesn't have anything to do with me, nor do I want it to. What you and Sadler . . .'

'But that's just it, Catherine,' Sophia cut in, her hand lightly touching Catherine's arm in an imploring gesture. 'There is no *me* and Sadler. Not that I haven't tried,' her dark eyebrows arched dramatically. 'I have, believe me.' She paused, taking a deep breath before continuing. 'Do you remember the day in the restaurant when we first ran into Sadler and you told me that you had been married to him but you divorced him?'

'I remember,' Catherine's lips barely moved. 'What about it?'

'I thought at the time that you must have been crazy to let anyone as gorgeous as Sadler to slip through your fingers, but . . .' Sophia shrugged, 'your loss was about to be my gain, or so I hoped, but it didn't work that way. Catherine . . .' her voice softened to a whisper, 'I'd give my eye teeth to have Sadler love me *one tenth* of the way he loves you.'

'You're the one who's crazy, Sophia,' Catherine swallowed tightly. 'Sadler doesn't love me. If you can't get to first base with him it's not because of me.'

'Yes, it is!' Sophia's eyes snapped. 'And any woman who spends more than ten minutes with him knows it. Oh, they might not know who the other woman is, but they know there is one. Women are always going to find Sadler attractive, that's a simple fact of life. But that doesn't mean he feels the same way.' Her rich full lips curved into a smile. 'Not *yet*, anyway.'

'What do you mean *not yet*?' Catherine couldn't stop the question from popping out.

'I mean,' Sophia's expression hardened, 'that Sadler

can't wait for ever for you to come to your senses.'

'Me?' Catherine was so angry she could barely get the word out.

'Yes, *you!*' Sophia snapped back. 'Personally, I don't think you've got enough sense left to realise what it is you're tossing away. But one of these days, Catherine, Sadler's going to give up waiting and let someone catch him. It's inevitable,' she frowned. 'Maybe it won't be me, but it will be someone.'

If Sophia was up to something, Catherine couldn't figure out what it was and her green eyes narrowed suspiciously as she stood there staring at Sophia. 'I still don't understand why you're telling me all this, Sophia. Especially if you're in love with him yourself.'

'Before Sadler came along,' Sophia's voice faded slightly, 'I thought you and I had the beginning of a pretty good friendship. I know that's impossible now because Sadler's still in love with you,' she shrugged, 'and I know you're still in love with him. So let's just consider this a friendly piece of advice—for old times' sake—and *wise up*, Catherine. Do something about Sadler, because if you don't you'll lose him for good.'

The door to Catherine's apartment shut behind her with a forlorn-sounding echo. It was the hollow kind of sound that only comes from knowing there was no one in the apartment—no one but herself.

The large oval mirror in the hallway caught her reflection, and like two strangers staring at each other for the first time, Catherine stood there staring at herself. The woman she saw was dressed in a crisp navy summer suit with a ruffled white blouse, accented at the throat with a small red silk rose. The woman's navy blue wide-brimmed hat had the same red rose on its band. With a thin smile she removed the hat and hung it over the mirror, blocking out her reflection. She had to do that because the woman looked as if she was about to say something, and right now Catherine was in no mood to listen to another lecture. Not even from herself.

She hung her suit neatly in the closet, then changed into a pair of jeans and a faded blue sweatshirt. She had considered going out for something to eat after the wedding, but somehow a celebration dinner with only one wasn't much of a celebration, so here she was, wandering aimlessly around the apartment, her mind stubbornly refusing to let go of the events of the day.

Smitty . . . Maggie . . . the wedding. That brought a smile, until she thought of who had given them their two weeks all-expenses-paid trip to Hawaii. Sadler always was generous—you could never fault him on that one.

Sadler . . . Sophia . . . Catherine threw herself down in the big chair by the living-room window, drew her knees up to her chin and stared bleakly into the rapidly approaching dusk. Maybe they weren't a twosome yet, but if the look on Sophia's face was any indication, she wasn't through trying yet.

Her nerves wound up almost to the breaking point, Catherine began pacing from the living-room to the kitchen and back, but her thoughts refused to give her a moment's peace. It was strange, she thought, that in a way Maggie and Sophia had both given her practically the same advice. But what if they were both wrong; what if Sadler had already washed his hands of her?

Ever since their weekend at the cabin things had seemed to get out of hand, and Catherine didn't know what to do about it. Once she had cooled down she knew Sadler hadn't purposely set out to take advantage of her, but by that time it was too late, everything had already been shouted. In the end when you're forced to admit that the position you've taken is completely indefensible, how do you keep justifying defining it? The answer was simple—you don't.

Loving someone doesn't mean never having to say you're sorry. It was more important then than ever. Catherine subconsciously squared her shoulders. Someone had to make the first move. No, she shook her head, not someone . . . *she* did.

Catherine's hand trembled visibly as she reached for the phone. What if Sadler laughed? What if he didn't say anything at all? What if Sophia answered the phone? Catherine dialled Sadler's number and listened to the phone ring three times, each ring jarring her nerves. After the third ring she heard Sadler's voice say, 'This is Sadler McQuade. I'm unable to take your call at the present time. At the sound of the tone leave your name and message and I'll get back to you.'

A recording machine! Catherine momentarily lost her nerve and started to hang up. then changed her mind and returned the phone slowly to her ear. Maybe this way was better. She could say what she wanted to without worrying about his reply. 'Sadler . . .' she paused; what *did* she want to say? 'This is Catherine,' she paused again. 'I'm sorry.'

She paused yet again, and as she did a tiny smile of relief formed on her previously tense lips. Having said that, the rest seemed so easy and she knew exactly what she wanted to say. It had worked for her once before— would it work for her again? 'Sadler . . . will you marry me—again?' A thousand words, a hundred promises swirled around in her mind, but they weren't things that needed saying now. Later perhaps, but not now. Everything important had been said—the rest was up to Sadler.

While Catherine waited for Sadler's phone call, she fixed herself a light snack, but who could eat when your whole life was hanging on one phone call? She waited, and waited and *waited*. Ten o'clock—eleven o'clock, and still no phone call. Even if Sadler had taken Sophia out to dinner after the wedding he still should be home by now. But what if he didn't go home? Catherine's heart sank. What if Sophia had given it one last desperate try and this time succeeded?

It was just after midnight when the doorbell rang, and

with heart-stopping certainty Catherine knew who it was. Brushing away any traces of dried tears from her cheeks, she held her breath as she opened the front door. 'Hello, Sadler.' It was a very soft, very uncertain greeting and matched perfectly by the expression on her face.

'Hello, Catherine.' *Catherine*, not Cat. Was that a bad sign? She couldn't tell. Sadler stood very tall, very dark and very solemn. 'I got your message.' And very concise.

Of course he had, she frowned, why else would he be here now? But why was he *here*? Why hadn't he just returned her phone call? That seemed like another bad sign to Catherine and she struggled to rid herself of the dry lump that had suddenly appeared in her throat. 'Come in, Sadler.' Stepping to one side, she watched him walk past her, his blank expression clueless as to what he was going to say. But after waiting for hours she couldn't wait one more second. 'Well?'

'Before we get into all that,' he sounded almost blasé about everything, his tall frame towering over her, 'I want to ask you something.'

'OK.' Her face pale, her stomach in knots, Catherine meekly agreed. What choice did she have? 'What is it?'

'Why now?' His grey eyes darkened. 'I mean that was a real cute message—not to mention being a big surprise. But why now, what prompted it?'

Catherine's heart sank. 'I don't know if I understand your question,' she swallowed hard. 'Are you asking me why I called you, or why . . . I asked you to marry me?'

'That's the one,' he nodded. 'Feeling a little nostalgic after the wedding today?'

'Well, I . . .' Catherine twisted her fingers nervously, Sadler's expression still not giving her a clue. 'Because you . . . because I . . . Oh, hell, Sadler!' her eyes flared. 'What kind of a question is that? Why does anybody ask anybody else to marry them?' She thinned her lips and glared at him. 'I want your money, of course.'

'I see.' The change in Sadler's expression was minuscule, but Catherine saw it and got the impression that he wanted to smile. It was almost as if he was enjoying her discomfort. 'Well,' he shrugged indifferently, 'at least you're honest.'

'That's *not* why, Sadler!' She gritted her teeth in place of stamping her foot. 'Why do you make me say things like that?' She drew a deep breath. 'I asked you to marry me because . . .' her voice faded, 'because I love you and I want us to try it again.'

'OK.'

Catherine looked more confused than ever. 'OK what?'

'OK, we'll get married.' It *had* been a smile he was hiding and it spread rapidly into an expression of tender understanding. 'Did you think I'd say no?'

'Yes!' Her eyes widened instantly. 'I did. I really did—especially when you took so long getting back to me tonight. The longer I waited the more certain I was that Sophia had . . .' She stopped talking and thinned her lips. Somewhere, in all the time she'd spent tonight waiting for Sadler to call her back, she had made several promises to herself—and Sadler.

'Sadler?' Catherine's voice was a soft plea, and he instantly reached out for her, but that wasn't what she wanted. 'No,' she shook her head and stepped back, staying just out of his reach, 'I have to say something to you, and I can't if you're going to start touching me.'

'All right, Cat.' Sadler seemed to understand that and dropped his hands back to his sides. 'What do you want to say?'

'After I called you this evening,' she swallowed dryly, 'I had a lot of time to think about everything, and I decided that if we were lucky enough to have a second chance I'd do a lot of things differently.' He reached for her again, but she shook him off. 'No, Sadler, please, let me finish.

'I know now,' she continued, 'that I was wrong about a

lot of things, and I'm going to change. I won't be jealous any more,' her forehead puckered slightly, 'or at least I'm going to try very hard not to be. I won't whine and complain when you're busy with business. I'll stay home and . . . learn to knit, or something. I'll control my temper,' she vowed. 'I won't get angry at silly little things. I . . .' Her green eyes suddenly narrowed. Here she was, being as serious about anything as she ever had in her life, and Sadler was laughing at her! 'I don't see anything funny, Sadler,' she snapped angrily, and promise number three went sailing out of the window. 'I'm trying to tell you I'm going to change, and you're standing there laughing at me!'

'Kitten, kitten, kitten,' he pulled her suddenly rigid body into his arms, 'I'm not laughing at you. It's the image you're projecting with all those wild promises. Knitting?' he laughed again. 'If you stuck to *half* of those promises you'd be dull as dishwater and I'd be bored to death in ten minutes. You wouldn't be you.'

'But—but—' she stammered, 'I made such a mess of our marriage the first time around that I want desperately for it to work this time. I was jealous and childish and . . .'

'It *will* work,' he promised, kissing her lightly on the mouth. 'We both know what we did wrong and I'm sure we won't do it again. And if you want to talk jealous,' he thinned his lips, 'you haven't got the market on that. Every time I turned around lately there you were on some jerk's arm. My jaw has been permanently locked for two weeks!'

Catherine's eyes gleamed with surprise and pleasure. That was the only time Sadler had ever admitted to that particular weakness, and she was delighted to know it existed. 'But they were never . . .'

'I don't want to talk about them,' he shook his head. 'They're not important. What is important is us. And as long as you're making promises I want to make a few of my own. I made a mistake keeping you in the background while we were married.' He stood back slightly, holding her in front of him at arm's length. 'I think it's time you had a hand in running McQuade Enterprises.'

Speechless, Catherine could only stare, her eyes gleaming like shooting stars. But like a shooting star that burns brightly for only a moment, her expression too began to fade. 'After the mess I made at Parker's you want me to get involved with electronics?' She shook her head dourly. 'Are you anxious to go out of business?'

'No, and I'm not going to.' His grey eyes darkened. 'You've got a good business head on your shoulders and I'd be a fool not to take advantage of it. You made mistakes with Parker's,' he admitted with a slight grin, 'a couple of doozies, in fact, but I know you're smart enough to learn from them.

'Catherine . . .' he paused, his fading smile an indication of a more serious subject, 'I didn't buy Parker's for the stock. I would have stepped in regardless. I made a mistake by waiting too long to approach you about it, but I honestly didn't believe you'd accept my help unless your back was right to the wall and you had no other option.'

'You're right, Sadler,' she smiled, twining her arms around his neck. 'I wouldn't have.'

'Good! And now that that's all settled,' he held her closer to his body, 'are you all packed and ready to go?'

'Packed?' She hadn't even considered it. 'No. Where are we going?'

'We're booked on the milk run to Reno,' he grinned. 'That *was* a sincere proposal of marriage on my answering machine, wasn't it?' He lowered his chin and nuzzled her ear, producing a giggle. 'Or,' he whispered in a seductive voice, 'we can chuck convention and live in sin for a while?'

'I'll be packed in ten minutes,' she told him quickly, resting comfortably in the circle of his arms. 'That is, I will if you'll let me go. How much time do we have?'

'You mean until the flight?' He sighed reluctantly and

let her go. 'Or how much time will we have together for our second honeymoon?'

'Both,' she nodded. 'But answer the last one first. A couple of hours, a couple of days, what?' It didn't matter to her what Sadler answered. She was going to accept it—be grateful for it—and keep her mouth shut about it.

'Ah . . .' he shrugged apologetically, 'the best I could come up with one such short notice was,' he paused and glanced at her from under his lashes, 'two weeks.'

'Two *weeks*?' Catherine couldn't believe him. 'Two weeks?' she repeated. 'Just the two of us on a *real* honeymoon this time? No combination honeymoon/business trip to San Francisco? No middle of the night East Coast calls? No people dropping in on us with incredibly rotten timing? No . . .'

'No!' He silenced her with a hard kiss on the mouth. 'You weren't the only one doing some thinking this afternoon after Smitty and Maggie's wedding. I couldn't help but remember our wedding, and *our* honeymoon—such as it was,' he shook his head regretfully.

'I know,' she whispered, 'I was thinking the same thing at their wedding.'

'You were?' He looked genuinely surprised. 'Every time I glanced at you you were so cool and your expression was so remote that I had the feeling you'd finally managed to put that part of your life behind you and forget all about it—and me.'

A sob caught in Catherine's throat as she realised how very close she had come to losing Sadler for good. It had taken Sophia to make her see it, but now that she had she wasn't going to lose Sadler again, ever, and she threw her arms around his waist, holding on to him as if her life depended on it.

'Hey!' he smiled tenderly, picking up her chin and kissing her softly on the lips. 'This is all very nice, and I heartily approve, but shouldn't you be packing? I can't promise more than the two weeks, but that much is ours—I swear to that.'

Catherine smiled and swallowed happy tears. 'Where are we going for our honeymoon?' She started for her bedroom, afraid to leave Sadler behind for even a second, so she pulled him along by the hand. 'Some place hot?' She glanced over her shoulder as she reached up on the closet shelf for her suitcase. 'Some place cold? Some place in between?' It didn't matter to her, anywhere was fine as long as they were together.

'I don't have any idea,' he shrugged. 'That's totally up to you. If I don't know where it is we're going, I can't have a moment's weakness and leave a number where I can be reached. So,' he grinned broadly, '*you* decide.'

'Anywhere I want to?' Catherine sat on the edge of her bed and looked thoughtful.

'Anywhere at all,' he restated. 'You pick the place. Surprise me. We can stay in Reno if you'd like, or fly on to Hawaii maybe, or . . .'

She shook her head. She knew exactly where she wanted to spend her honeymoon. 'I want to come back here to West Virginia after we're married and go up to the cabin. Can we do it? Will your friend let us borrow it again?' Her voice bubbled with happiness and growing enthusiasm. 'Oh, but if we do that,' she continued on a sober note, 'it will mean there's someone else who knows where we are. Will he promise not to tell anyone?'

'Bill doesn't own the cabin any more, Cat.' Sadler looked very sombre. 'He sold it.'

'Oh?' She was crushed but tried not to show it. 'Well . . . OK. We'll have to go someplace else, that's all,' she shrugged. She stopped talking and looked at Sadler. His expression had changed from sober to the cat-that-ate-the-canary look. '*You're* the one who bought it!' she accused. 'But why?'

'I had to,' he shrugged. 'I had a big investment in food left up there. I could hardly let it all . . .'

She jumped to her feet, throwing herself at Sadler and knocking them both off balance. Instead of trying to stop them both from falling, he gave in and directed his fall towards the bed, conveniently taking her down with him. 'Now see what you've done,' he whispered, his grey eyes coming alive with a warmth she recognised.

'But I've got to pack,' she protested weakly, momentarily catching her breath as his hand slipped up under her shirt and across her bare back. 'We've got to go. We haven't got time to . . .'

'We've got the time,' his voice was low, husky and slightly muffled as he nibbled at her lips. 'We've got all the time in the world.'